For Hannah C.

This one was yours from the beginning.

OF THE WILD

WILD

E. Wambheim

OF THE WILD

WILD

E. Wambheim

Copyright © E. Wambheim, 2021

Cover design and illustration by Hannah Culbert

First paperback edition June 2021

ISBN 978-1-7357532-0-1 (paperback)
ISBN 978-1-7357532-1-8 (ebook)

I

UIET NOW, his earlier wailing no more than an echo, the infant cradled in Aeris's arms gazed up, unblinking, at the myriad of faces peering down at him.

"What will he look like?" one of the other children asked. Her tail curled around Aeris's wrist. "I bet he'll get feathers."

"Horns," hissed another, and "Big, big scales," came from a third. The bets flew fast, then—a gathering susurration of excitement over their newest sibling. Those who couldn't fly or climb tugged at the sweeping hem of Aeris's night-black cloak and begged to see.

At the rising noise, the baby's face crumpled, and Aeris could hear, just at the edge of sound, the high, high whine that

1

proceeded a proper howl. The infant's cheeks, already rosy, turned tomato-red.

"I hear you, sweetling," Aeris whispered, soft and smooth, as the baby's mouth screwed into a puckered frown. Tiny hands emerged from the cocoon of blankets, equally tiny fingers curling and uncurling into weak, waving fists.

"What's he doing?"

"I can't see him--"

"What's he doing?"

Aeris cradled the new baby against his chest and seated himself cross-legged to give the watchers on the floor a better view. Those perched on his arms and shoulders shifted to keep their balance. The rest of his family clambered over his gleaming black boots to settle in and around his lap. Small claws and talons caught in the velvet of his breeches, but he whisked away the damage with a thought.

"The noise startled him." He swept a half-serious frown over those he could see, but all eyes were on the baby. The infant blinked, newly-quiet, and Aeris had been so unable to stop smiling that he fell easily into doing so again. "We have to speak softly until he is used to us."

One of the small, fat-fingered hands patted against the thick grey fur of the child nearest, and though someone gasped in excitement, no one squealed or shouted. A three-fingered hand returned the contact and nestled into the baby's wispy brown hair. The baby gurgled, and Aeris's smile wavered.

"They left him crying," he began, and another silence fell, this one tight and anxious. "They left him crying tonight—and for too many before. They left him hungry and frightened."

None of the children spoke. Aeris lifted his dark, dark eyes from the new baby to take in the children clustered around him. Mira, once half-drowned, now grey but alive, the dark slits of gills stark against the pale curve of her neck. Orion, covered in the thick, rough-edged scales that had grown over his cuts and bruises. June, her hands bent and broken beyond what magic could fix, her knuckles soft with moss and a fuzz of white flowers. Eris, sprouting pale blue mushrooms on his bare shoulders and down his back, their clustered caps glowing enough to shed a weak, watery light in the black depths of midnight.

In total, his children numbered twenty-three, now twenty-four, each one plucked from rain-swept doorways or fished out of old sacks or lifted from cold and careless houses. The forgotten, the unwanted, the unloved. So many of them smaller than they had been in life, their bodies compressed and twisted into whatever shape they thought would keep them safe. Too many with beaks and claws and fangs. Too many with shells and scales and ridges of bone.

"They wanted a baby who did not cry, who did not fuss. They wanted a baby who would not wake them in the night. So," Aeris continued, spinning his voice back into levity, "I left them a stone. They shall see it as their child and never know the difference."

That sent a shimmer of laughter through those gathered. In his lap, the baby squirmed, and Aeris nestled him on the floor between two of his fluffier siblings.

"He may be *terrifying*," he went on, to another, stronger spate of giggles. "With great, gleaming eyes for seeing in the dark. Or horns—here and here." He pressed his fingertips against Orion's forehead—and Orion squirmed away with a bubbling laugh. Aeris rocked forward, scooped up Mira, and swung her into the air. "Or rabbit legs," he announced over her sudden peal of laughter, "for bounding over your head."

As he set her back down, tiny, crooked hands and claws reached up, each owner begging for their turn to be tossed, but Aeris swept over them with a finger to his lips. "Or fluffy ears," he whispered, tugging gently at the tips of his own, "to hear everything. Those might grow in first. So rest now and keep quiet, so he does not fret again."

"Did anyone see you?" This from Aimee, who crouched nearly behind him, so that Aeris had to lift his arm and peer around the edge of his cloak to see her properly. Her tall, tufted ears lay flat against her skull, and she kept her paws tucked in her lap, hidden from sight. "Is anyone going to come looking for him?"

Between his new siblings, still in his nest of blankets, the baby had closed both huge, bright eyes. Aeris brushed a thumb through the mused brown hair.

"If either of his parents come to claim him," he began, quiet and serious and storm-cloud dangerous, "they will have a steep price to pay for what they have done, and very, *very* few find they want to bargain with a creature of the Wild Woods."

II

THE PARENTS DID NOT COME.

The Tall Ones did.

Aeris smelled them before he saw them, their scent a wash of spearmint sharp and stinging. His children smelled them, too: all around the glen, they froze and dropped into the grass with ears flat or fur on end or eyes wide and yellow. Those with wings or sturdy claws retreated to the high, spidering branches of the Home Tree. Only the baby, cooing in the fallen leaves at his knee, remained oblivious.

They did not so much appear as drift into focus between the autumn trees. One looked much like the other: stretched tall, of course, and twig-thin with pale purple skin and dragonfly wings. They clustered on the far side of Aeris's border, and Aeris could feel, like an itch beneath his skin, their testing of his magic.

In a single motion, he rose and sprang for the border, twisting into bat—badger—panther—then something all raised hackles and wicked claws. "Go away," he growled. "Go *away*."

They laughed. The nearest one, his eyes eggshell-white, favored Aeris's wild shape with a smooth and perfect smile. "Aeris," he began, and the charm dripped off his words like honey, "we came to see your newest little one."

He could feel them testing the boundary still, and he bared his teeth, sent a new flood of *pass-not pass-not pass-not* into the border.

"Aeris." Another smile, another laugh, this one still full of a bell-like sweetness. "If you steal them so, you cannot be upset when others think of doing the same."

"He is not for the taking," he managed, speaking with a mouth increasingly ill-equipped for speech. He wanted to spin into a storm, into thunder and lightning and thrashing rain. "*None of them* are for the taking."

"And your claim? They are not your kin. You have no ties."

"Their home is here. Their home is with me."

"If you wanted halflings of your own, you needed only a willing mortal."

Aeris gave no answer but a growl, the crack and rumble of it tearing through his chest and throat. *Pass-not pass-not pass-not,*

7

he insisted again, this time with force enough to send the nearest stumbling back. Behind him, safely distant, one of his children blew a raspberry.

The Tall Ones laughed again, and this time the sound was harsh and grating. "Keep them for now," one said, as the foremost, mocking, tapped a finger to his chest. "We all measure your time, Aeris, and it shortens."

They faded, then, drifting out and out and out of focus until they vanished altogether. An autumn breeze pulled scarlet leaves from the canopy and sent them twirling like wild sparks into the moss and undergrowth.

Aeris remained stiff-legged at the border. Their scent faded until he could smell nothing beyond earth and encroaching rain and decomposing leaves.

A rustle in the air above him, then in the grass beside, snapped his attention away from the trees. Bess crouched beside him, her white-and-black feathers flared in a ruff around her neck and all down her back. She tugged, uneasy, at the grass underfoot.

"Are they gone?" she asked, her voice hardly more than a whisper. She turned midnight-blue eyes to his. "Did you win?"

Aeris swept back into the shape most welcome: human but for the ears, his dark hair loose around his shoulders. He opened his arms, and Bess flew up at once, crashed into his chest, and dug her claws into the fabric of his coat. He wrapped her in a hug, as tight as he dared given the hollow fragility of her bones, and carried her away from the tree line.

"They have gone," he promised, fierce still, simmering still. Slowly, slowly, he let go, let go, and properly softened. He touched his nose to the ruff of her feathers. "They have gone."

"Did they want the baby?"

"Yes."

"Well, they can't have him."

The infant in question squirmed his pile of leaves and batted at the brightest, crumbled them between inelegant fingers. Aeris settled beside him once again, Bess still in his arms and nuzzled close against the curve of his neck. "They have gone," he said again. "They shall not get him, sweetling. Not him nor any of you."

Around him, gradually, his children eased back into motion. He could hear the scratch of talons on tree bark as climbers made their way down from the Home Tree; a few, from the sound of muffled laughter and the *thump* of feet on the earth, simply jumped down instead. A game of catch-me-if-you-can rekindled, drew its players back up into a whirl of giggles and giddy abandon.

Some, however, darted across the grass to sit with Aeris instead, to shelter under the fall of his coat or to wedge themselves into the shelter of his arms and each other. Amaya, with a tiny growl, crouched down beside the new baby; Pel resettled his wings beneath his carapace and pulled the edge of Aeris's coat around his iridescent shoulders. The rest jumbled in his lap or as close as they could manage, and Aeris murmured over and again, "They are gone. They are gone. They are gone."

III

WE ALL MEASURE YOUR TIME, AERIS.

He traced the grooves of the Tree's rough bark, the edges catching at his fingertips. The nighttime orchestra of crickets and the deep, soft breathing of his sleeping children filled the hollow Tree with a peaceful music. Each of them lay curled within their alcoves, wrapped in blankets or sleeping warm without. Drifting wild-lights lit the inverted bowl of the ceiling with a warm and flickering glow.

Outside, the Tree towered above Aeris like a jagged black shadow against the sky, old and twisted, with bark so weathered it seemed more stone than wood. Wind stirred its bare branches, and with the breeze came the first whisper of winter.

Aeris could feel against his palm the Tree's sluggish crawl of life. The churning river of magic once pulsing beneath the bark had slowed to a trickle, and life wavered with it.

11

He closed his eyes and pressed his forehead against the Tree's stony bark. *Please*, he begged—not as a spell, not as a magic, just as a prayer. *Please, not yet.*

IV

HORI WOKE HIM THE NEXT MORNING with claws on his coat and a whispered, "Dani! Dani! There's something outside."

He sat up in the darkness, rubbing sleep out of his eyes. "What manner of thing?" he asked, likewise at a whisper.

"A ghost—I think it's a ghost. Please come look."

Aeris could hear the rest of his children sleeping still, all twenty-three breathing slow and steady. Hori shivered at his knee, either with the predawn chill or with fear; Aeris picked him up and pulled his coat closed around him.

"Where is the ghost?" he asked, and Hori squirmed a wing out from beneath the coat, pointed bone and membrane and a hooked claw toward the sliver of forest visible beyond the Tree's threshold.

The ghost stood on the edge of the glen, just beyond the shield of Aeris's magic. Human-shaped and barefoot, he hunched

13

his shoulders as if cold, and he kept his hands in the pockets of his soft, shapeless clothes. He held his head tipped to one side, as if listening for something, but the forest around him was deathly-quiet.

Aeris watched him from the mouth of the Home Tree, and the ghost's gaze, grey and puzzled, settled upon him. Hori tucked himself out of sight with a squeak, but Aeris stood unwavering, his shoulder propped against the edge of the threshold, his body a shield to keep his family from sight.

"I would like to speak with this one, sweetling," he whispered, pulling open his coat just enough to address Hori. "Would you like to stay here or come with me?"

"Come with you," came the muffled reply, and so Aeris stepped from the shelter of the Tree into the moonlight and crossed to the border for the second time in as many days.

"What are you?" he asked as he drew nearer, and he let a chill curl through his voice. Nothing wandered this way, not without reason, and those reasons were not always gentle. "What do you want?"

The ghost did not seem to hear. "Where are you?" he asked, and his voice sounded far away, heard from the other end of a tunnel. "Where am I?"

Up close, the ghost's edges kept shifting, as hazy as dispersing mist. Short, curling hair carried a faint tint of gold, and one cheek was shadowed purple, as if with a bruise.

"Are you dead," Aeris asked, "or dreaming?"

"Dreaming, I think." A blink, a flicker of a sleepy sort of bemusement. "I hope I'm not dead."

"What brings you dreaming here?"

Another blink, and the ghost's eyes seemed to focus, his gaze still on Aeris's face. "Are you okay? What's happened to your eye?"

Aeris jolted a step back, startled, and instinctively threw out a *see-me-so* for dark eyes, for a high-boned and elegant face, for silver earrings glinting like stars. "I can see you," he retorted, then tried again, voice steadier: "My sight is as it should be."

"Oh?" The ghost's expression wavered. "Where am I? I've never been here before."

"Well," Aeris replied, still unsteady, his heart a drum in his throat, "you are dreaming, then, and here by chance. Wander elsewhere. "

But the ghost stayed where he was, confused and barefoot and hunched against the cold. Aeris watched him as he flickered in and out of focus. The purple of his bruise stained his cheek almost black.

Lost. This one was lost. Too old to take in, but lost all the same, and what was this glen but a shelter for those adrift?

Aeris eased forward a step, caught the ghost's gaze deliberately this time. "Find this place by daylight, not by dream." Softer now, gentler now. "Come away."

The ghost's expression slid into a frown. If he heard, or intended to obey, he gave no sign. The fraying edges of his shape spread, unraveled him further, and within the space of a breath, he disappeared. Aeris waited until his heart resumed a calmer beat, but the ghost did not return.

As he strode back toward the Home Tree, Hori poked his head out from beneath the collar of Aeris's coat. "What did he mean, something happening to your eye?" he asked, his own wide and glossy-black. "Both of 'em look fine to me."

"Who can say, sweetling. Human sight is often unreliable."

"Hm." A wrinkle formed across the bridge of Hori's upturned nose. "Is he bad?"

"I think not," Aeris began, "but if he moves to harm, he is a locust, and I will change him so. Then one of you may eat him for breakfast."

Hori considered this for a moment, ears upright. "I wish you could do that with the Tall Ones that come by. I don't like them."

16

"I wish that, too." Aeris favored him with the embers of a smile, grateful for the solid, familiar weight of one of his children settled against his chest. "But they would taste terrible: hard and bitter."

That earned a giggle, if a quiet one. "Like eating a *stick*," Hori whispered, and his voice was full of theatrical disgust. "A dried-up dead one."

"Just so." As he stepped back into the Home Tree, surrounded now by the rest of his safe, sleeping children, Aeris's smile flared to a brighter life. "Thank you for waking me, little bat," he murmured as he helped Hori detach from his clothing and clamber up into an alcove. "Sleep well and dream well. I shall see to the rest."

V

EVEN AFTER THREE DAYS, the baby's skin remained soft and pink; his eyes, though doe-like in size and color, remained human in shape and scope. He showed no sign of growing new teeth at all, let alone fangs or venom sacs.

"When's he going to look like us?"

"What's he gonna have?"

"Maybe he's growing in claws, and they're just growing in real slow."

Aeris said nothing, and as the baby only blinked and burbled at the small, strange crowd gathered, did not dissuade his children from their curiosity. The infant had wrapped a pudgy starfish of a hand around one of Aeris's fingers, and he swung the tiny hand back and forth, marveling as always at how frail and helpless humans were at the start. Frail and helpless but voracious—something small fighting from its first breath to learn and see and grow.

Warm in a wash of autumn sunlight, with this new life in his lap and his children in a messy pile around him, the Tall Ones and their threats felt like a distant nightmare. Sen hung over his shoulder for a better view of the baby, and Finn wedged himself beneath Aeris's arm for the same. Amaya ignored all of them, interested only in chewing one of the buttons off of Aeris's coat, and Aeris felt a fierce, fierce love for all of them twisting so tightly in his chest that he almost could not breathe. His dear ones, his beloved little monsters.

Kira propped herself on one of Aeris's knees and stuck her muzzle against the baby's cheek. With a muffled, damp snuffling, she investigated him from ear to hairline. "He still smells different," she complained. "Like cars and smoke and things. Not like here."

"Perhaps he has not yet decided to stay with us." Still made soft by an overflow of fondness, Aeris wriggled his finger in the baby's grasp, not yet trying in earnest to pull it free. "Shall we feed him and see?"

Excitement ricocheted through those gathered, and the peaceful, curious mood sharpened. "I want to get it!" and "Let me get it!" and "No, no, I want to find it!" flew into the air like a flock of startled birds.

"Pel," Aeris cut in, smooth and level, "if you would, please."

With a triumphant buzz of blurred wings, Pel shot up toward the Tree's canopy, and the others watched with more eagerness than jealousy as Pel sought out the Tree's only fruit and returned with it cradled against his chest. He landed at Aeris's elbow, and Aeris lifted it from his outstretched claws with a "Thank you, love."

Like the fruit before, this one glowed scarlet between his fingers, its skin scaled like a raspberry and warm to the touch. But while most had been no larger than the nail of his index finger, this one was smaller still, and Aeris tried not to think on why.

As his family watched, all eyes unblinking, he flattened it into a rose-pink pulp. Crimson juice trailed down the curve of his thumb, as dark and thick as blood.

He reclaimed his finger from the baby's grasp and managed, clumsy with one hand and with children balanced on his head and shoulders, to scoop the infant into the crook of his arm. Without a spoon, he set the remnants of the fruit just behind the haphazard row of baby teeth.

"What does it taste like?" Pel asked, too young to remember, and Sen answered: "Sweet. Like syrup. And like a penny, too."

"Don't put pennies in your mouth," Finn whispered. "They're not for eating."

"*Anything* is for eating."

With infantile curiosity, the baby mushed the fruit against the roof of its mouth. He didn't make a face, and he didn't spit it out, and he stuck out the tip of his pink tongue as he swallowed.

"He ate it?" Sen dug her fingers into Aeris's collar as she leaned closer to the baby. "He stays?"

"He stays," Aeris promised, and satisfaction brushed through those gathered like a late summer breeze, a breath exhaled. Kira stuck her nose against the baby's cheek and sneezed.

"What's his name gonna be?"

The answer rose, as usual, before Aeris could consciously give it shape: "Mika."

"Mika," Finn parroted back, and Aimee patted the baby's forehead with a soft, "Hello, Mika."

If Mika recognized that he had been named, that he had been formally brought into the fold of a new family, he did not indicate as much. He bubbled a laugh and managed, after a few failed attempts, to wedge three of his own fingers into his mouth, and Aeris marveled again at how mortals started life as something so small and doughy and soft. As fragile and precious as a baby bird hatched too soon.

His heart in his throat, Aeris swept Mika properly into his arms and dusted a kiss against his forehead. "I shall keep you safe, sweetling," he whispered, and the words were as much a promise as a blessing. "Welcome home."

VI

DREAMS WERE THE PURVIEW OF HUMANS, but Aeris drowned in them all the same. Drowned in the Tree empty, every hollow a gaping hole, the air stale and deathly silent. The smooth wood had cracked, turned raw and bleeding, and as Aeris tried to press the wood whole with a *heal heal heal*, great flakes of it came away in his hands.

"Stop," he pleaded. *Stop.*

The Tree crumbled against his hands. A heartbeat slammed against his ears—the desperate drumming of a cataclysmic death. His own heart stuttered in his chest like a frightened bird. *Stop stop stop—please stop.*

Blood coated his hands. He dropped—not to the Tree's floor but to soil thick with rain and rotting wood. "Stop," he gasped again. "Not this. Not yet. Please, not yet, not yet--"

He woke. Woke to the cool, dark, ruffled peace of the Tree alive and alive with the shift and sigh of those at rest. Everyone asleep. Everyone safe.

With no one to see, Aeris closed his eyes and placed a hand over his heart. He could feel the swell and sink of his chest with each breath, but his pulse was a weak, distant flutter against his fingertips. He was tired—so tired.

Not yet. He folded both hands over his sternum, pressed down as hard as he dared. *Heal heal heal please heal.*

But his heart continued to beat faint against his palm, a moth caught in the bowl of his hands. The skin of his chest felt rough and rigid, even through the fabric of his shirt. He touched his jaw, his cheek; the same roughness snagged his fingertips. His hand, when he lifted it and risked a glance, wore the wrong shape, his fingers thin and crooked—claws in the dark.

Not yet. He curled his hands against his chest, ignored the way his fingers nearly refused to bend, willed his body back into human shape. Fought against the exhaustion that pulled at his worn and weary body like an implacable tide. *Please not yet.*

VII

"BE A BIRD! BE A BIRD!"

Raven. Aeris twisted into a streak of black feathers. Hands and paws reached up to catch him, but he cawed a laugh and circled out of reach. Before those with wings could follow him into the air, he dove and swept over his audience to shrieks of laughter.

"Butterfly!"

"Rabbit!"

"Mouse!"

He managed something all three: curled antennae and whiskers and soft black fur. But he'd made his hind legs too long and, off-balance, he tumbled ears over tail into the fallen leaves. He bumped against a knee (one so sharp it must have been Sorrel's) and arms hooked around his middle to haul him upright.

"A bear!"

25

"Yeah, Dani, be a bear!"

Mindful of the bony arms around him, he surged into a larger shape. He heard a squeak from beyond his shoulder, but Sorrel caught hold of the fur on his neck and held tight.

His children whooped and scrambled forward in a tumult. Two grabbed one of his paws, hauling on the pads as if trying to tip him over. Others simply seized the fur on his legs and pulled themselves up onto his back. Those short enough to do so ran under him, the tops of their heads skimming the fur of his chest.

Mindful of the disarray of those clinging to him and those underneath, Aeris dulled his claws and took one wide, heavy step—and ignored the pinch of a dozen hands twisting into his fur to keep their balance.

"Stand up! Stand up!"

"Stand up!"

A whiff of smoke and asphalt.

Aeris froze. Those were city smells. Human smells.

He did stand, the short muzzle of his bear-shape tilted to catch the source. His still-shouting riders drowned out any sounds the intruder might have made, but they gradually grew quiet and watchful as they realized Aeris had stopped playing.

He caught the scent again as the breeze shifted, and he caught, too, an unfamiliar pool of gold and amber between the trees.

As the children, too, spotted the stranger, they dropped from Aeris's legs, and Aeris swept back into human form, into a black velvet coat with deep pockets, soft boots for silence, no jewelry save his silver earrings. Only Sorrel remained on him, her arms looped around his neck. His eyes still on the stranger, Aeris knelt so that she could drop down, and then rose again, striding across the clearing to stand guard on his side of the border.

The stranger stood halfway behind one of the maple trees just at the edge of the clearing. He'd dressed in black and faded autumn orange, as if with half a mind toward camouflage, but as Aeris approached, he edged out into the open and stood with his shoulders hunched and his hands in his pockets. Freckles scattered like spilled cinnamon across his face; his ruffled hair, gleaming in the afternoon sun, had been the gold that gave him away.

They faced each other across the invisible line of Aeris's shield, Aeris with his children whispering behind him and the stranger with nothing at his back but the rattle of wind in the fallen leaves. One eye wore a dark, plum-purple bruise, and a deep, still-bleeding cut ran along the bone of his cheek.

The young man glanced away. "You told me to find you," he growled, defensive, as he hiked his shoulders higher. "What do you want?"

Aeris tilted his head to one side. Here stood a tomcat, stiff-legged and fluffed with false bravado, though Aeris could see in him, too, the gently-puzzled ghost of before. "What do *you* want?" he asked in return, voice soft.

"What makes you think I want anything?" came the immediate rejoinder, and Aeris found his gaze met by one green eye and one brown: eyes to see both worlds. No wonder his dream-sight had been so sharp.

"Who did that?"

"Who did what?"

Aeris touched his own cheek with one finger, traced a line that mirrored the cut trailing down to the young man's chin.

"Oh." The stranger's fingertips touched the cut. His knuckles were as bruised and bloody as his cheek. "Nobody," he insisted, and his mouth twitched into a deeper frown. "Just some asshole."

"*Some asshole,*" someone whispered from behind Aeris. He turned and found Sen almost underfoot, grinning up at him from where she crouched in the grass.

"Some... jerk," the stranger amended, as Aeris crouched to hoist Sen into his arms. Mismatched eyes caught on the sandpaper skin of her arms, on the jagged teeth that stuck out over the curve of her bottom lip. "That's what I meant to say."

28

"*Asshole*," Sen said again, savoring the word. Then, "I'm a goblin," she added, quite nonchalant. "If Dani doesn't like you, I'll bite."

For a moment, the stranger said nothing, but as Sen bared her rows of shark-like teeth, pulling down the corners of her mouth to show off as many as possible, his expression softened. "My," he began, amused at some private joke, "what big teeth you have."

Sen's fingers wedged against her gumline rendered her reply incomprehensible, and the stranger's mouth hooked into a genuine, if crooked, smile.

Bruised hands, bruised cheek, bruised heart. Lost in some way that had led him here. Aeris could smell no magic on him, just shampoo and city smoke—no trace at all of the spearmint stink that marked the Tall Ones.

"What is your name?" he asked, and the mismatched eyes snagged on him again; the young man went still and watchful again.

"I'm--" A muscle tightened in the young man's jaw, as if he had to physically fight the urge to reply. But, "I'm Will—or William," he admitted at last. "You can call me that."

"William, then." The name felt too light on his tongue, all air and no substance. Not a lie, no, but a new address: not one from which Aeris could draw a claim. Aeris tilted his head again, this time in invitation, and, with Sen still bundled in his arms, turned halfway toward the sunlit clearing. "Shall we?"

"Shall we what?"

"Well, you walked all this way." Aeris favored his would-be guest with a smile. "Come see what you found."

With his jaw tight again, William seemed on the verge of refusing altogether. But as Aeris began his stroll back to the Tree, he heard the crackle of dry leaves as William followed. He felt, too, in the same moment, the disturbance in the border as William passed through: a shift in the air, an invisible hand brushing against the back of his neck.

The children (except, now, for Sen) had not moved from their cluster in the grass. Of those not present, Aeris knew without seeing that they slept still in the Home Tree; he could feel their peaceful, dreaming sleep in the roots of his thoughts. Those outside simmered in a different mood: cautious, but not afraid.

"Dear ones." Aeris drew to a halt; William, half a step behind, staggered to a less-elegant stop. "This is William, who is a strange visitor but not a bad one."

Yellow and grey and black eyes shifted from Aeris to the newcomer and remained there unblinking. William stared back, his gaze drifting from Finn's small, velvety antlers to Sorrel's bony protrusions to silver, beadlike scales to muzzles and claws and tree-bark skin. Watching him closely, Aeris waited for a recoil. Waited for William's dreamlike curiosity and uncertainty to twist into repulsion. He let *turn-him-stone* sizzle in his fingertips even as he knew, with a whispering certainty, that he would not need to spell him so.

William did not recoil—nor did he smile. Without his tomcat bravado or hunched shoulders, he seemed smaller—a stray, half-tame creature sniffing at the edges of new and unknown territory. With a thoughtful, distracted slowness, he picked first at his bloody knuckles, then at his cheek, pulling absently at the dried edges of his cut.

"Oh!" That from June, of course from June. She darted forward in a streak of white and silver. "Mine, too." She held up her hands for him to see. "Mine, too."

Aeris watched, unblinking and unmoving, as William crouched. But William did not tease, as he had with Sen, and he did not bite, as he had with Aeris. He took June's hands lightly, so lightly, in his and turned them over one at a time, took in with an unflinching sobriety the moss growing through the cracks in her skin. The flowers blooming between her fingers glowed as white as fallen snow against his bruised and bloody knuckles.

"What's your name?" he asked, so quietly Aeris almost didn't hear.

"June." June inspected his hands with the same closeness, her eyes as bright as new stars. "What happened to yours?" she asked.

"Someone was picking on a cat," he answered, his voice still quiet, still soft, despite the flicker of strong feeling in his words. "So I hit him. He hit me back."

"What happened to the cat?"

"She's okay. She ran off."

"Good." June freed one hand and patted the back of William's wrist—and that broke the stillness: Aeris let the unused spell fizzle out, and the other children crept closer to investigate. William held still, not quite smiling, as Amaya sniffed the laces of his battered shoes, as Pel landed on his shoulder to peer into the empty hood of his sweatshirt, as Lily pulled at the tattered hem of his jeans with an unfurled mantis claw.

"Are you gonna grow flowers, too? Or big teeth?"

"Why are you so old?"

"Are you gonna fit in the tree beds? What if you don't fit?"

"Do you like dogs?"

"*Am* I old?" William asked, as Amaya began to chew on his shoelaces. "I'm twenty-three."

Lily retracted her claws as if burned. "That's *so* old."

"Is it? How old are you?"

32

Aeris could have answered for her, but Lily only blinked. Her antennae and iridescent eyes did not lend themselves to human expressions, but Aeris could see confusion in the steep tilt of her head and the waver of her body from side to side.

"You are five by his calendar, sweetling."

"*I'm* two-hundred." Sen swung her legs against Aeris's ribs and drummed her hands against the collar of his jacket. "Tell him I'm two-hundred."

"And Sen says she is two-hundred."

A quick, crooked smile tugged at the corner of William's mouth—a sudden hint of gold amidst the stones of a riverbed. "I've never met anyone who's two-hundred before."

Amidst a swirl of "*You're* so old!" and "I'm *twenty-* hundred," and "You can't be; that isn't even a number," Aeris picked his way closer to William and, mindful of little hands and little feet, folded himself down beside him. William glanced in his direction, wariness now only in the crease between his eyebrows rather in the whole of his posture, and rocked back to sit cross-legged in the grass. Pel, still halfway into the hood of his sweatshirt, buzzed his disapproval as the movement swung him off-balance.

"Careful," Aeris whispered, but William stilled on his own, held himself motionless as Pel resettled and hooked a claw into the collar of William's shirt. "I can ask them not to climb on you, if you like."

"No, it's okay." Despite the young man's wince as Amaya's teeth caught the toe of his shoe, his answer carried the clean, crisp ring of truth. "Are all of them yours?"

They are not your kin. You have no ties. But this was not the mockery of the Tall Ones; this was a question asked in earnest, and Aeris shrugged the indignant lift from his shoulders. "Of course. Their home is here." His voice, despite the prickle of remembered ill-use, remained steady. "Their home is with me."

Sen squirmed out of his arms, then, and tripped over her own feet in her haste to land on Amaya. With a bark of surprise, Amaya tore off across the grass, Sen a shadow on her heels. At this revival of their earlier tousling, and with the new-penny gloss of William's presence somewhat worn away, most of those gathered took off to join the chase or to wrestle each other into the dead leaves. Finn tucked himself beneath the fall of Aeris's coat, snug against his leg and away from the noise, and Aeris rested a hand against the lump that was the little one's shoulder.

William watched the gamboling with the distant, bemused frown he'd worn upon his introduction. "What a weird dream," he mused.

"This is not a dream." The mismatched eyes settled on him again, this time with no shift in expression, and Aeris returned William's gaze with a polite and feigned disinterest. "Why do you think yourself asleep?"

William wrinkled his nose at the question. "I saw you turn into a bear. Your kids are growing mushrooms. I walked here from the *park*. Are you kidding? This *has* to be a dream."

"Your last visit was a dream. This one is not."

Though he shook his head, William did not otherwise answer. His eyes did not leave Aeris's face, but his gaze drifted inward, and Aeris could nearly see the last visit replaying in the young man's thoughts.

"Your eyes were all fucked up last time," William said at last. "*Messed up*," he amended, as Finn poked his nose out from beneath Aeris's coat. "They were *messed up*."

Sharp sight—and a strong memory. On instinct, Aeris checked the *see-me-so* on his face and his hands and his clothes, but the spell had not waned. "And what of my eyes today?" he asked, his voice tipped high with spun-sugar innocence.

"They're fine today." As if on cue, William turned back toward the clearing, toward the loose and wild game of catch-me-if-you-can tearing through the grass. The muscle in his jaw crimped again, and he asked, voice stilted, "Are they okay?"

35

"My eyes? Or the children?"

"Both, I guess." William tugged his sleeves down over his hands. "That girl, June. There's... scars. Under the flowers."

"Yes."

"I see," and William's voice had a new tenor: a storm-cloud simmer. "Are they all like that?"

A breeze mussed the young man's sun-bright hair, and leaves whirled around them in a swirl of scarlet and gold. (Shrieks of delight went up from the children as the wind whipped leaves around them, too.) With the sun on his cheek, William's bruise stood out all the more sharply against the paler backdrop of his skin. The wine-dark stain marked the edge of his cheekbone, drew a sharp edge upon an otherwise soft face. Freckled and scarecrow-ragged, he was beautiful in the bright, brief, burning way so particular to humans.

Aeris turned, too, to watch his children tumble across the clearing. "They asked to be somewhere safe." A handful parted from the chase and scooped armfuls of leaves into a steadily growing pile. "I heard them."

"They're all so young."

"Yes," Aeris conceded, then added, thoughtful, "and no."

"How old are *you*?"

Aeris favored William with a sideways glance and a careful, not-quite-teasing smile. "What would you guess?"

William didn't seem to notice the smile: his expression remained somber as he studied Aeris's face. "Twenty-five."

"Seventy," Finn added from his hiding place, and Aeris laughed at both guesses.

"Twenty-something? Am I close?"

"I would not know." Aeris swept a hand toward the clearing, toward the Home Tree at its heart. "This place does not age as you do."

"So you're old." William's mouth crimped into a pinched, puzzled frown. "And you can turn into animals. What are you?"

Aeris tilted his head at that. William wanted a name, a title, an answer clean and clear and easy, but Aeris had no such answer to give. What was he? A pest, a welcome visitor, a fleeting miracle. Something neither human nor truly Wild, not like the Tall Ones, and not quite like his children either.

"I am of the Woods," he said at last, and laughed as William rolled his eyes. "And I am a friend. What other answer would you like?"

"*You're* the strange one." But William's voice carried no cruelty, only a sort of reluctant acceptance. "So you've adopted all of these kids? None of them are yours by-- by blood?"

37

"Not by blood, no." Aeris knew what he referenced: tumbling and heated caresses—a life-creating ritual older than any of them, human or Wild. He shrugged, dismissive. "What that would require, I do not care for," he replied. "I have no interest in or love for any part of that process."

"Oh?"

"But," Aeris went on, *not your kin* an unwelcome echo in his thoughts, "they are no less my children for that. I am their guardian, and they have my heart—the whole of it."

William watched him, his frown thoughtful. His interjection had sounded more intrigued than surprised, but "You're *sure* I'm not dreaming?" he asked instead.

"Quite so."

"And *are* you okay? Your eyes, I mean."

"Did you not call them fine?" Aeris asked, hoping to deflect the question, but William did not take the bait, and simply waited, focused and unblinking. Unable to lie, unwilling to tell the truth, vividly aware of Finn awake and attentive at his side, Aeris tried again: "Which do you think is true: what you saw in your sleep or what you see now?"

William broke neither his gaze nor his silence. Under such a focused stare, Aeris felt exposed and pulled apart, an apple half-peeled. Despite the nervous trip of his heart in his chest, he kept his breath deliberately deep and slow, his expression placid.

Eventually, William relented and looked away, raising one hand to pick again at the cut on his cheek. "Why did you call me here?" His voice turned soft and careful, almost tentative. "What do you want?"

Aeris shook his head, tried to slow the rabbit-kick of his pulse. "This place is a haven for the lost, and you wandered to it. The question is, William, what do *you* want?"

"No." William's tone, though still soft, deepened into surety. "No, I heard you. I remember you from when I was dreaming; we talked somewhere over there." He gestured, vaguely, toward the stretch of trees that had been the site of their first conversation. "But before that, I heard a voice—your voice—and I followed it here."

"Mine?" A ribbon of unease unfurled in Aeris's stomach. "What did I say?"

"The same thing, over and over: 'Please. Not yet.'"

Aeris froze. *Please.* The press of his forehead against the Tree's rough bark, his heart sick. *Please, not yet.*

William's eyes were on him again, and Aeris's stomach lurched. He was a butterfly pinned, surprise a stake through his chest, his alarm as visible as veins on a wing. William had heard him.

William wouldn't know—*couldn't* know—what Aeris's plea signified, but he had heard it, and as panic caught Aeris's heart back up in a frantic tattoo, he was suddenly, blindingly afraid William would hear that, too, would see him with and without his thin veneer of magic, would know the shape of him in an instant.

"Okay." William's voice reached him as if from far away. "Okay, I don't think you wanted to hear that." Bruised hands fluttered in his direction, then drew back. "Sorry. I didn't mean-- I'm sorry."

Aeris felt Finn shift against his leg, and as he began to wriggle out from beneath Aeris's coat, Aeris drew in a deep, shaking breath. With two sets of eyes on him, one discordant and the other doe-brown, he managed to school his expression into something approaching calm. He would not be seen. He would not be known. Not here, not now.

"I'm sorry," William said again, and Aeris could tell both from the tilt of his voice and the twist of his hands that he apologized in earnest. "I didn't know I wasn't-- I didn't mean to freak you out."

Aeris opened his mouth to reply—but a "Whoa, look at it!" from across the clearing caught his answer in his throat. "It came right out!" followed on its heels, and both Aeris and William snapped to attention.

Sen scrambled toward them with a string of her siblings trailing behind. She brandished something white and triangular between two fingers, waving it over her head like a battle trophy.

"It fell right out!" she called, all excitement. "Look how big it is!"

Aeris, already on his feet, met her halfway and dropped into a crouch. Sen smacked her prize into his waiting palm, its edges sharp against his skin. At the sight of it, Aeris's earlier panic folded and gave way to a wave of sheer, dizzying pride.

"Darling!" He laughed, delight a champagne fizz in his chest. "You lost a tooth."

Sen grinned, and Aeris held the tooth up to the new gap in her smile. Her siblings jostled her from either side, talking over one other in a rush: "I saw it go," and "I found it in the grass when it fell out," and "Are the others loose? Are they loose right now?"

Despite the new flurry of noise, Aeris still heard the faint shuffle of leaves behind him. He turned without rising, took in William standing stiff and uncertain, his balance shifting from one foot to the other in the wake of an extinguished need for action. Finn sat near his shoes and tried to reknot one set of fraying laces.

"Dani? Can I have my tooth back? Can I keep it?"

"Yes, of course." Aeris returned the tooth, and Sen cradled it in her palm to better show it off to her siblings. "And it is time

41

for William to leave, so let us bid him farewell."

June, near the front of the group, turned shining eyes on William. "You're leaving?"

William, when Aeris shifted again to look at him, was watching him in return, his hands once more in his pockets and his expression carefully blank. "Seems like it," he conceded, and Aeris's heart leapt again, as frantic in his chest as a caged bird. This was Aeris avoidant, and both of them knew it.

"Your visit is appreciated." Aeris rose, voice steady, hands steady, gaze steady. "You may visit again another time."

June darted forward to squeeze William's hand in a quick farewell, and Finn tugged on the hem of his jeans with a whispered, "I fixed your shoes." William responded to the former with a gentle press in return and to the latter with a soft and serious, "Thank you." To those not distracted by Sen's lost tooth, he waved, and continued waving, even as he backed toward the edge of the clearing and his path home.

Aeris hung back, safe in the midst of his flock, but even at a distance, he caught the shift in William's expression as he reached the tree line: from blank to something wistful, something almost hungry. And then, with one final flicker of a glance in Aeris's direction, William turned and strode through the barrier and vanished into the shadows of the gilded forest.

VIII

MOONLIGHT FLOODED THE MOUTH OF THE HOME TREE and pooled silver on the smooth wooden floor. A midnight wind howled through the forest beyond, but the Tree retained a warmth and stillness incongruous with the weather outside.

Aeris sat with his back against the inner curve of the Tree, his hands folded in his lap and his eyes fixed on the boundary between clearing and Wild forest. Exhaustion unraveled the edges of his thoughts and left him less than half-lucid, but sleep slid through his fingers like smoke.

He could see Mika's fluff of golden-brown hair tucked between two sets of darker curls; the twins flanked him, their rabbit legs tucked partway beneath the blankets. One mumbled in her sleep, then burrowed closer and relaxed again with a tiny sigh, and Aeris's heart swept into his throat, as it always did, at the sight of

43

them so quiet and drowsy and soft with trust. These were his children, and this his patchwork of a family, stitched together from scraps and strangers and splintered hearts.

This home was a haven and he, guard and guardian both, would keep it so. Of course he would keep it so, but--

I heard you.

Aeris tilted his head back against the curve of the Tree and stared instead at the hollow vault of its ceiling. William flared in his mind's eye, tense and tousled and bruised, and Aeris pushed the image away with a weary determination. *No,* he insisted to no one, to the tumult of his own churning thoughts. *He has no role in this.*

But William had *heard*. William had wandered the woods in search of Aeris's voice—and found him. Why had a human heard him? Why had *anyone* heard him?

"He should have no role in this," Aeris insisted again, this time aloud, as if speaking the words could make them true. "He claims to want nothing."

And yet--

And yet--

Aeris saw, again, William gently, so gently turning June's hands over in his own, his knuckles bloody, hers soft with moss. The thin crack of his smile. That last, wistful glance. The sunlight

44

on his bruised cheek and in his hair, its glow turning him bright and beautiful and fierce, fierce, fierce.

That's why. Aeris closed his eyes, let hope and fear and sorrow settle stone-heavy in his chest. *That's why he's here.*

IX

Morning dawned crisp and clear, and Aeris stepped toward the trees with his breath a fog and his shadow a stretch of lingering midnight.

He glanced over his shoulder into the dark shelter of the Home Tree. Some of the early risers stretched in their alcoves, and a few eyes glowed at him from beneath drawn blankets, but most slept heavily still. *Sleep*, he pressed, and the gleaming eyes closed, the first stirrings of the morning resettled into stillness.

Sleep would hold. The barrier, too, would hold, even if the Tall Ones appeared, for once, before noon.

When he heard new children, their cries for help were more sensation than sound. He could feel them knotted in his chest, a tethered string pulling and pulling and pulling. Birds found their southern nest, sea turtles found the sea, and Aeris found the scared and the small.

He felt no such pull toward William, and so Aeris folded into dog shape: sleek black fur, spindly legs, a thin and tapering muzzle—and a nose so strong that the sudden tumult of new smells left him dizzy and almost ill. He paced through the fallen leaves, nose to the earth, until he found the day-old tang of smoke and asphalt and gasoline, of soap, stale bread, and sweat.

His heading thus, Aeris padded into the Woods proper. This deep in the forest, William's scent ran weak but steady, and Aeris followed the trail across a carpet of crackling leaves, around snarls of bramble and wild rose, beneath the arching branches of oak trees broad and twisted. He crossed over a shallow creek, not even ankle-deep, with stones scattered from bank to bank and water as clear as clean glass. The city smells grew stronger on the far side, and Aeris flicked his ears up as he loped from the shaded shelter of the forest to the empty expanse of a city park.

The grass pricked sharp at the pads of his paws, and the air felt thicker and somehow dusty; it filled Aeris's lungs like smoke, and he sneezed. Cars trundled along roads out of sight, and their growling engines sounded like an alien language—indistinct and indecipherable. A few early runners kept to the park's sidewalks, their shoes a regular *tap tap tap* against the pavement.

Aeris lifted his nose to the air and could smell a woven map of the city. Car exhaust wove between restaurants; coffee and cigarettes marked the passage of the day's first commuters. But even with the new sensory onslaught, he could pick out, still, the trace that was William, threadlike and thin.

With his ears angled toward the roll of traffic and his tail in an easy swing, Aeris trotted through the park and onto the sidewalks beyond. He kept his distance from the street, the fur of his shoulder brushing brick and concrete as he slid from shadow to shadow to alley to shadow again. The humans he passed spared him no second glance, and as Aeris wove around sneakers and polished leather, he needed only the slightest *see-me-not* to turn all but invisible.

The Tall Ones hated cities, hated any landscape so altered by humans and so full of forged metal, but Aeris found human dwellings to be hazy with magic of a different style. Nature here might have been domesticated, hemmed into neat squares and window boxes, but the Wild had too-sharp of teeth to be so contained, and it crept out of smoke and sewer grates to tangle with humanity in a way those of the forest never could. As long as Aeris kept to his own business, so too did the breathing city.

William's scent gradually grew stronger, and with it grew a knot in Aeris's stomach, a lump of root and vine that twisted all

48

the way up into his throat. Perhaps he not find William—and the prospect of turning back toward home left Aeris momentarily dizzy with guilt and relief. He could still turn away. He could leave the city with his pride intact.

His pride—at the cost of twenty-four lives.

So Aeris kept his heading, claws clicking on the concrete, and wound his way deeper into the city. Buildings shifted from old brick to glass and steel to brick again. As the sun crept higher, Aeris found his way onto streets crowded with houses and apartment buildings. Grass fountained up from cracks in the sidewalk, and the concrete slabs hitched against one another as if buckled by an earthquake.

Soap, stale bread, sweat—all three, now, bound up with coffee and old wood and dust. *Here.* William's trail veered from the sidewalk to the doorway of a brick building with a battered front door and tired, stick-like flowers in what might have been a garden. The building's two full rows of windows were closed and shuttered, but the topmost—a narrow rectangle tucked by itself beneath the peaked angle of the roof—stood open.

Aeris slid easily from dog to raven and launched skyward. He hooked his talons into the wood of the window ledge, resettled his feathers, and cocked his head to peer into the room beyond. He could make out little in the semi-darkness, only the steep, sloping sides of the ceiling and a mattress, strewn with blankets, wedged against one wall. A thin beam of light, hazy with motes of dust, fell across curled fingers and golden hair, but the rest of the sleeper remained buried beneath the pile. But Aeris did not need to see the sleeper's face; he recognized the color and curl of the hair, the healing cuts across the knuckles.

Aeris croaked a greeting and wedged his beak against the edge of the window screen. He hadn't managed to do more than rattle it when William lurched upright in a landslide of blankets. Alarm disappeared from his expression in the space of a blink, and the protective hike to his shoulders slid away. He adjusted the neck of his T-shirt, pulling it even at his collar, and dug the heel of one hand into the bruise on his cheek.

"The front door," he rasped in a voice scratchy with sleep. "Go on, if it's you," he added, when Aeris only tilted his head. "Don't come in here."

With another croak, Aeris turned and hopped off the ledge. He spun into human shape as he neared the ground so that he landed light-footed on the sidewalk, and his coat floated with a smooth and gentle elegance down around his shoulders.

A set of cement steps led up to the building's front door, but a flash of doubt snagged in his thoughts, and Aeris drew back a pace. He could still leave. He could still try to manage on his own.

Perhaps he had not failed, only made some overlooked but reparable mistake.

The protests, even to him, sounded weak—a last scramble for leniency against a tide too strong now to swim against. He could, he could, he could—but no. He had made his decision the night before, and he would not shirk from it now. Whatever the cost, Aeris would pay it.

So Aeris held himself resolved and stepped up to the foot of the stairs, clasped his hands behind his back, and waited.

When the lock of the front door *ticked* open and William edged out onto the doorstep, Aeris caught a glimpse behind him of five or six coats hanging from a three-legged coat rack, scarves looped over and around them in a fretwork of plaid and blue wool, before the door closed. And then William filled his vision instead, dressed again in the same faded orange sweatshirt from before, his feet bare and the mess of his hair crushed beneath a knit cap. He rested his back against the closed front door, one hand still on the knob.

"Come with me," Aeris began, before William could speak. As much as he knew he ought to soften, he squared his shoulders, stiffened into cold formality. "You are needed in the Woods."

William blinked and straightened. "You want me to come *back*?" he asked, disbelief plain in his voice and in the lift of his eyebrows. "But I fucked up."

"Did you?" Aeris hesitated and lost his stoic countenance in a surge of confusion. "How so?"

"I mean-- I swore like ten times and told your kids I beat up some guy, and then I freaked you out so badly that you asked me to leave." William's voice wavered on the last word and he coughed out a humorless sort of laugh. "It was a *great* first impression."

Oh. Guilt twisted tight and wire-thin in Aeris's chest. He stepped forward and touched a hand to the railing of the short flight of steps. "You did nothing wrong," he insisted, conciliatory and honest in equal measure. "You surprised me, and my response is my own. Do not hold yourself responsible for my reaction."

William looked unconvinced, and as Aeris ascended another step, he dug his free hand, a fist, into his pocket. "Whatever you think I can do, you'll find someone better. Keep looking."

"No." Another step up, three of the four. "No one else will do."

"Oh, yeah? Why?"

Aeris studied him for a moment. William did not glow in the watery morning light as he had in the afternoon sun, and his battle-wound of a bruise had faded to a sickly yellow-green. Here, in this element, he seemed ordinary—as plain and human as any other person in front of any other house in any other city.

A human and a stranger and woefully mortal, and yet--

And yet William had sought him out.

When Aeris felt the tug of a call, he followed it without knowing where he would go, whether to the tiny square of an apartment or to a farmhouse bordered by nothing but acres and acres of corn. He went without knowing who called or what he would find or anything at all beyond the one thing that mattered: someone needed his help, and he would not turn away.

William had done the same. William had heard Aeris's distress and, knowing nothing beyond that, beyond the echo of *Not yet*, had sought him out.

"Because," Aeris began, low and smooth and certain, "you have the heart for it."

Still skeptical, William tilted his chin in the barest hint of a challenge. "The heart for what?"

"For looking after my family."

"For-- Oh." William's hand slid from the doorknob. He blinked, and something in his expression sharpened, as if his thoughts jumped into focus. "'Looking after' as in...?"

William's too-bright gaze pinned him again, and Aeris looked away at once. "I am dying," he admitted, his heart in his throat, "and they will need a guardian."

"Oh." An exhale—a soft, surprised sound. "That's... kind of a big thing to ask."

"It is." Aeris tipped into formality again, lifted his chin for a regal bearing despite the anxious patter of his heart. "And I am here to beg or bargain or bend to such an arrangement as you find suitable."

"To... what?"

"To beg."

"God, no, I don't think you have to *beg*."

"To bargain, then." He could not help the hardening of his voice, the sharp edge not of reluctance but of resignation. He touched a hand to his chest. "Take part of my magic or take part of me—take *something* as payment for the adoption of this mantle."

From the corner of his eye, he saw William sink onto the top step and prop his elbows on his knees. The young man slid a hand beneath his hat to twist his fingers into the riot of his hair; at that, Aeris risked a proper glance over, but William pushed his face into his hands and did not look up.

"Okay," William muttered, his voice muffled by his palms. "I think this might be a sit-down kind of conversation."

Aeris did not, for the moment, sit. He had come prepared to sell himself in pieces, to bargain away bits of his soul or what remained of his magic, and the possibility that William would refuse utterly, would refuse even at the promise of restitution, left him cold.

But as William slid his hands off his face to peer up at him, and as Aeris did not know how else to proceed, he edged up onto the top step and knelt beside his would-be replacement. William shifted sideways to give him more room, and they sat side-by-side with space enough between them for a third person to pass through.

"Right. So." William twisted, turned toward him, leaned forward with his elbows again on his knees, his hands poised for added emphasis. "I would be a shitty guardian."

"Not so."

"Yes so."

Aeris might have mimicked William's pose to communicate the same intensity, but he kept his hands folded in his lap. "Not so," he insisted and, as William scoffed, softened his approach: "Why do you persist in that claim?"

"Because it's true." As soon as the words were out of his mouth, William flushed, and the blush suffused the whole of his face, turning him rose and gold. "I'm not..." He cleared his throat, pulled at the scabs on his knuckles. "I'm not a great example of how to grow up."

Growing up? A smile tugged insistent and surprised at the corner of Aeris's mouth. "They do not need to learn how to grow up," he said, almost with a laugh. "They need someone to care about loose teeth and old scars. And someone to keep them from eating dead spiders." William's frown turned puzzled at that, and Aeris saw him, in a flash of memory, as the washed-out ghost on the edge of the glen. "They need," he went on, "someone who knows what it is to be lost and found."

For a long moment, William said nothing. He stared at a crack in the sidewalk and picked at his injuries with a meditative slowness. Aeris watched him, watched as the rising sun threaded into his hair and turned him copper.

Eventually, William's gaze, emerald and earth-brown, flickered back to him. "What are you dying of?" he asked, his voice as quiet and careful as the shift of his attention.

The urge to retreat hooked in his thoughts, sent him instinctively scrambling for a way to turn the question back—to twist his way out of an answer—but, "The Tree is fading," Aeris replied, matter-of-fact, "and I fade with it."

"The what?"

"The Tree. You will see it if you come back."

"Why? I mean, why are you tied to it like that?"

That was perhaps not answered so easily. Aeris could not remember now which of them had come first or if there had even been a time before they had been so tied. The Tree's magic and his, the Tree's life and his—whatever laced them together bound them as deep as root and bone.

"It is the way of things," he said at last. "We have always been so."

William's answering "Hmm" sounded more thoughtful than annoyed. He touched the cut on his cheek, ran a finger along its ragged edge. His blush had receded, but his cheeks and nose remained pink, and Aeris remembered only then that William wore neither shoes nor a coat.

"Are you cold?"

"Oh? Yeah, I guess." William glanced down at his arms, then his feet, as if he'd forgotten them. He pulled his sleeves down over his hands and wedged his palms beneath his soles to shield them from the cold cement. "I'm sort of used to it. I don't have winter clothes yet."

"None at all?"

"Not yet, no, but it's okay."

Six coats hanging empty on the other side of the door and none of them his, not even to borrow for the space of a conversation.

57

Aeris unfolded himself from the step, shrugged out of his velvet coat, and—as William sat up, startled by the movement—draped it with a flourish across the young man's lap.

"There." He dropped down a step and flashed William a smile he didn't quite feel. "You may make use of that one."

"Oh, no, I can't-- No." William scrambled to his feet with the fabric bundled in his arms. "I can't take this: it's yours. "

"It *is* mine," Aeris replied, backing down the steps even as William tried to push the coat into his hands, "and I may share it as I like. If you want to return it, you know where to find me."

That arrested him. William stiffened, that now-familiar wariness winding his shoulders tight, but this was not a trick, and Aeris did not mean it as one.

"Come once more. Just once." A gentle voice, a gentle nudge of the coat back into William's arms. "Choose then."

For one beat of his heart, then two, Aeris thought William would push him away, him and the coat and this last request. But then the young man readjusted his hold on the coat, tucking it more securely against his chest. "Okay," he whispered, almost too softly for Aeris to hear, and the word hung in the air between them, a golden promise. "Okay. One more visit."

X

FOR THE WHOLE OF THE NEXT DAY, shifting orange and gold kept catching at the corner of Aeris's eye, but each time he turned to look, all he could see were leaves falling and sunlight gilding bark and branch. The sun ambled along in its slow arc overhead, and Aeris glanced over his shoulder again and again, hoping for a glimpse of William's approach.

But William did not come, and he did not come, and he did not come. As the sun began to set, Aeris's fear that William would not appear turned to dread that he would: the Tall Ones prowled the Woods at their leisure, and Aeris did not know if they were more likely to ignore William or to steal him.

Dusk darkened the edges of the glade and left a prickle of cold in the air. His children darted after drifting wild-lights and tried to catch them in the cups of their hands. Light sparked on scales and claws and yellow eyes, and Sen's mouth glowed like a jack-o'-lantern each time she managed to stuff a wisp into her mouth.

Aeris kept out of this game and sat instead between the huge roots of the Home Tree, the stone-solid trunk a reassuring pressure against his shoulders. Mika lay bundled in his lap, Bess perched on his knee, and Eris leaned against his hip, all three of them bathed in the soft blue light of Eris's mushrooms. Bess kept teasing Mika, tickling his nose with the tip of a wing, then fluttering out of reach each time he giggled and tried to grab her feathers.

Despite the bright mood and the ruckus, Aeris felt drained and hollow, exhausted either from waiting or from yesterday's surfeit of magic. Was William lost? Had he forgotten his promise? Or had he changed his mind? If so, what then? Worry stretched his heart into string, and Aeris did not know how to wind it back into shape. He wanted everything to slow and calm and soften. He wanted to sleep. He wanted to tilt back into the embrace of the Home Tree and dissolve into the trunk and the leaves and the tangled roots, into a sluggish, thoughtless pulse of life.

"Oh! You're back! Hello!"

"Dani has a coat just like that!"

Aeris flicked his eyes open (how long had they been closed?) just as the shiver of the barrier disrupted brushed cold against the back of his neck.

William—William at last—picked his way through the last of the underbrush and into the clearing proper. His hair gleamed a polished red-gold in the last of the sun; the cut on his cheek shone scarlet. He carried Aeris's coat over one arm, and as Amaya and Pel reached for the trailing ends of it, he swung it up and out of reach.

"This isn't yours," he chided, playfully serious in a way Aeris had not heard from him before. "I'm giving it back to its owner."

Amaya swung an arm in a futile attempt to reach the coat, but Pel shot upward with a fizz of his wings. William lurched backward, startled. Pel crash-landed against his chest, and William's hands came up—either by instinct or reflex—to catch him, and Pel dropped with an "Oof!" into the cradle of his arms.

"Are you okay?" William sounded breathless with surprise and concern. "Are you hurt?"

Pel hooked one of his spindly second arms beneath the coat. "Got it."

William blinked, at a loss, and Pel met his uncomprehending stare as he slid the coat the rest of the way off William's arm and into Amaya's waiting paws. Amaya snagged the

61

coat and tore off across the grass with the black fabric billowing over her head and several of her siblings on her heels.

Aeris rose, then, with Mika propped against his hip. Eris tucked himself into the vacated hollow, but Bess launched herself after Amaya, and Aeris paused long enough to pick up one of her dropped feathers before he strode across the clearing to welcome his guest properly.

Though his mouth had begun to tilt into the start of a smile, William sobered as Aeris reached him, and he straightened as if expecting a reprisal.

"Hey. Sorry I'm late. I--" He broke off with a swallow, as though he had thought better of whatever he intended to say. "Yeah. Sorry."

"You need not apologize." Relief had Aeris grinning. William was neither lost nor inconstant, nor did he seem annoyed by Pel's trickery. Even now, he stood with Pel still in his arms, not as if he'd forgotten he was there but as if his weight was no burden at all.

"But it's late. You might have gone to bed. I didn't--" William broke off again, this time as his gaze tripped down to the bundle in Aeris's arms. "You have a baby now?"

"You did not meet last time, but he is not a new arrival." Aeris stepped closer, bringing Mika up against his chest so that

William could see him properly. "This is Mika. We are waiting still for his new traits to grow in."

"I want him to have horns," Pel whispered. "Big curly ones."

"Aye, love, those would suit him well."

But William did not seem to be listening. He leaned over Mika to see him better, his shoulder wedged against Aeris's and his curls tickling Aeris's cheek. Aeris could smell soap and the citrus tang of shampoo, moreso than the sweat and stale bread of before. William did not seem to notice their new closeness: he gazed, silent and serious, at the liquid brown eyes blinking up at him. Mika had stuck two of his fingers in his mouth and seemed more interested in this new pastime than in his surroundings.

"Do they always start out like this?" William asked. "Like... regular?"

"Not always so young, but yes."

William said nothing, and Aeris could not see his face. Pel tried to pinch the strings of William's sweatshirt in his claws, but if William noticed, he did not intervene. Even with Pel in his arms, he ran his thumb along the knuckles of his forefinger, and Aeris wondered if he was seeing the baby at all, or if his thoughts had turned elsewhere, back toward June and scars under flowers.

When William finally straightened, his expression was deliberately blank, but Aeris did not miss the tension in his stance or in his curled hands. He knew that anger; he knew the temptation to claw and bite and burn.

"I find the children," he began, and William's blazing eyes snagged on his, "and I get them out, and I do not go back."

"Why not?"

"I lose the way." Aeris could no more return to a visited home than he could reach the moon. Without the pull from a child lost, he navigated with no compass—and the temptation to bite, to spread like a plague through the other rooms, could never in the moment eclipse his impulse to rescue and soothe and spirit away.

William's mouth creased into a deeper frown. His arms tightened, apparently unconsciously, around Pel, who grunted and began to squirm. "You're squeezing me," he complained, kicking his heel against William's wrist.

"I'm what?" William blinked—and the storm cloud of his mood vanished in an instant. "Oh! Shit! Sorry." He relented, already bright red with embarrassment as Pel buzzed up into the air. "Are you okay?"

"*Shit*," Pel echoed, amenable again now that he was no longer being crushed. He landed on William's shoulder, just long enough to bump his forehead against William's temple, and then launched himself after his siblings in a noisy blur.

With his arms now empty, William didn't seem to know what to do with them. He started to tuck his hands into his pockets, stopped, began to pull his sleeves over them, stopped, then raked them through his hair where he left them twisted into his curls.

"*Is* he okay?" he asked, his voice high and thin. "Did I make it worse?"

"You did not hurt him." When that did not catch his attention, Aeris tilted his head to be in the young man's line of sight. "William. There is no harm done."

"I told you. I *told* you I'd be a shitty guardian."

"How so? He protested, you listened."

William did not answer, nor did he turn his gaze from the dusk-dark shapes tousling over Aeris's coat. Someone (from the bark of laughter, probably Amaya) was being rolled into the coat by her siblings, and William watched them with the same wistful, almost-hungry expression he had worn upon his last departure.

"William." Aeris gave the young man's shoulder a nudge with his own and pretended not to notice the way William startled back into the present. "Come. See the Tree."

"Yeah." Then, more steadily, "Yeah, show me."

Near-forgotten worry flooded back into Aeris's stomach. He turned and led the way to the Tree, trying for the first time to see it as an outsider. How would it look to William? Like a grand

and ancient part of the forest? Or like a dead thing, some broken shell best left to dust?

Eris's blue glow had vanished from the roots; the only illumination came now from the thin, tree-broken band of sunlight on the horizon and the golden flicker of wild-lights from within the Tree itself. Aeris picked his way over the shadow-black sprawl of roots and paused in the mouth of the Tree to wait for his guest.

William approached with identical care, pausing just within the reach of the roots to tip his head back and take in the skeletal canopy of branches overhead. When he drew closer, he stepped on none of the roots, only on the bare earth between, and even with the low light, he did not trip. He came to stand beside Aeris, the pair of them shoulder-to-shoulder in the threshold, and brushed the fingertips of one hand against the coal-stained stone of the Tree's bark.

"It's sick?" he asked, his voice little more than a whisper.

Aeris did not answer that, only said, "Come see the rest," and ducked into the Tree proper. The shouting of his children faded at once—audible still but muffled.

William followed, as if by instinct, and Aeris watched his gaze shift from the Tree's bark to the wooden floor inside to the alcoves empty except for their tousled blankets. He glanced upward, and the reflections of the floating wild-lights caught in his eyes: the smallest fallen stars embedded in moss and earth.

"There's room enough? For all your kids?"

"Of course. There is always enough."

"How many kids do you have?"

"Twenty-four."

"Have you always had twenty-four?"

Aeris tilted his head to one side, trying to hear the question that wasn't being asked. William, still focused on the lights above, did not even so much as glance at him, but Aeris could feel the prickle of his attention like static against his skin.

"Not always," he answered, deliberately vague, but William did not press further, and silence settled between them like dust.

A fresh bout of laughter erupted outside, and Aeris took an automatic step toward it. He tilted his head, listening more closely, but no one cried, no one yelled. The pilfered coat had not yet turned into something to be fought over.

Leaving William to his silent perusal, Aeris withdrew and sat on the edge of the Tree's hollow, his feet propped against the roots outside. The children had resumed their hunt for wild-lights, and those who could not fly darted like leaping shadows in the gathering dark. Beneath their hoots and cackles, he could hear William padding light-footed through the Home Tree.

Without the Tree, what would happen to them? Would the barrier hold? Would there be a home for them here, even if it did? Aeris could recall too easily the wood cracking apart beneath his hands, the choking stink of rot and rain-bloated soil. What home would they have if the Tree splintered?

Aeris exhaled and closed his eyes. Fear was a seed he could not allow to take root. He could imagine it small and rock-hard in the pit of his stomach, something to be buried too deeply to sprout. Whatever time he had, no matter how much or how little, he would not be afraid. He would not be insufficient.

The patter of William's steps changed, and Aeris opened his eyes in time to see the young man settle cross-legged beside him, not quite close enough for their shoulders to touch. The wild-lights cast a faint, candlelight glow upon his hair and skin. His expression, as he looked out over the clearing, was closed and tight—a bottle too full to risk opening too quickly.

"How can you be so sure?" he asked, and Aeris did not need him to clarify what he meant. "What if you're wrong?"

"Do you want me to be wrong?"

"No, but--" William broke off and put his hands to his face. After a moment, he sighed and skated his fingers up into his hair and left them buried. "But I'm not a good choice. I mess up. I mess up a *lot*. And I break things—and I really, really don't want to break *this*."

At the breathless fear in his voice, the knot in Aeris's chest unraveled. *I am not wrong* rose to the tip of his tongue, but he did not answer so. "Do you want to be here?" he asked, as gently as if asking one of his children.

For a long moment, William did not answer. He kept his face half-hidden behind the shelter of his arms, his only movement the rise and fall of his shoulders as he breathed. Aeris sat beside him and, after a stretch of silence, pretended to be wholly absorbed in tickling Mika's nose with Bess's lost feather. Mika warbled and giggled, and the sound joined the tidal ebb and flow of shouted laughter from beyond their ring of light.

Then, at last, his voice so quiet that Aeris almost didn't hear him: "I want to be here. But I don't... I don't know." William's fingers curled into his hair, but he did not look up. "Your family's so weird and-- and charming—and I-- I don't know."

"Charming?" Aeris tilted his head so far to one side that his ear nearly touched his shoulder. "You find us charming?"

William's answering *tsk* might have been a laugh. "Yeah." He glanced up, the start of a crooked, uncertain smile edging his mouth. "Well, *they* are. I don't know about you."

William found his family *charming.* Pride and delight curled warm through Aeris, a pleasant heat shimmering into his fingertips, but his smile was all mischief as he asked, still canted sideways, "You do not find *me* charming?"

"No." A brighter crack of a smile. "You're trouble."

"Trouble? Me? Surely not."

"With a smile like that? Yeah, you are."

"How unjust." Aeris recoiled, mock-offended. "My children get to be charming, yet all I am is trouble."

That earned a half-hearted sort of laugh, and William untangled his hands from his hair to set them in his lap. He dropped his gaze to his healing cuts, and began to pull, restless, at the skin of his knuckles.

"You know those big family get-togethers?" he asked, and he might have passed for careless had his ears not already turned a bright, embarrassed pink. "The ones that have, like, thirty people all jumbled together in the same house?"

Aeris heard the catch in his voice and straightened. "I am not familiar, no," he admitted, soft and apologetic. "Tell me."

"Oh. Well." William shrugged; his blush spread rosy across his face. "There's always, like, at *least* ten people in the kitchen and ten more by the front door—and some of them still have their coats on, even after half an hour. And everyone else is crammed into the living room. It's always chaotic and warm and loud and... I mean, it's kind of awful, really. Everyone is trying to talk to you at once, and everything is hugs and hellos and coats just *everywhere*."

"That does not sound awful." Had Mika not been in his arms, Aeris would have touched William's hand, eased his nails away from digging deeper furrows into his skin. "William. That does not sound awful at all."

William hiked one shoulder up—either in a shrug or as a shield. "I know. That's... That's the kind of family I want to be a part of. That's the kind of family you have, and I just... stumbled into it. I really--" He broke off, his voice cracking. "I *really* don't think I deserve to be here."

Deserve? Both the word and the sentiment felt alien on Aeris's tongue, and he had the fleeting, fleeting impression of dancing, of trying to match William's steps without knowing his rhythm or his style. How did one *deserve* a family? How did one *earn* a family?

A pearl of new blood blossomed on William's cracked skin, and Aeris rocked to his feet. "Here." He pivoted to face William, Mika balanced in the sling of his arms. "Catch."

As fast as flinching, William raised his hands—palms out, as if he expected Aeris to toss Mika into them. But Aeris eased the baby down into William's arms (gently, of course), and even as

71

William leaned back, uncertain, he adjusted his pose and reached, palms up this time, to accept the small and squirming bundle.

"Keep his head supported. There you are." His hands now free, Aeris guided William's arms into more of a cradle and pushed on his hand and elbow until William drew Mika snug against his chest. "Keep him close to your body, just like that."

As Aeris began to withdraw, Mika gurgled and kicked his covered legs, and William drew in a sharp, sudden breath. "Don't-- Don't back up yet," he whispered. "What if I drop him?"

"You won't." But Aeris paused, his hands on William's, as Mika waved a tiny fist, the quill of Bess's feather clutched tight between his stubby fingers.

"I might."

"You won't." Aeris gave his hands a muted squeeze, pressed certainty and steadiness into his skin with nothing more magical than human sympathy. "Give yourself a chance."

William exhaled rather than argue. His skin was dry and cratered against Aeris's palm, and Aeris could feel the thrum of William's pulse against the edge of his smallest finger. He nearly laughed at the irony: William was not afraid of his children, only afraid of hurting them.

Slowly, slowly, the tension unwound from William's shoulders and his expression softened, if not into a smile, then into something like a cloudy day: subdued but with sun behind. "The last time I held a baby," he began, "was right after my niece was born, and she cried until I gave her back to her mom."

"You have siblings, then?"

"Just one. An older brother."

"Is that not a family you would regret leaving?"

"No." William's hand curled beneath Aeris's, just enough for Aeris to feel the shift of bones beneath his palm. "I've already left."

"Is that who you live with, in your house in the city?"

"No."

Aeris waited, curious, but William did not elaborate. Behind him, he could hear someone cheering, "Sen! Sen, I got another one!" and an unintelligible shout in response. "These sleeves are *so long*," came from somewhere on the other side of the Tree. "I can't find my hands." Aeris closed his eyes and tried to walk in the wake of William's steps, tried to understand the shape of a mind where family was *deserved* or *undeserved* and not simply *given*.

"Family," he began, sharply aware, even with his eyes closed, of William's drawn attention, "is the garden that grows you before you realize you are growing. It is the dirt and the sun and the air, and you take root where you can, even if all you have is stone and shade.

"And if that first planting does not take, we try again." He blinked, found William's eyes on him, their green and brown as dark as deep water in the gathering night. "In a different garden, we try again."

For a long, stretched-out moment, William did not reply. In the inconstant light, his expression verged on the inscrutable, but Aeris could feel the slow unfurl of William's hands beneath his own.

Then, "I was wrong," William admitted at last, his voice all gravel. "You *are* charming."

"Ah. You learn quickly."

William coughed a laugh, or something like it, and began to stand. "Here," he croaked, proffering Mika. "Catch."

Though close already, Aeris straightened and stepped forward. William's hair brushed his cheek and Aeris caught again the soap-and-citrus smell of him as Mika changed hands. Then Mika was in his arms, reaching for a loose ribbon of Aeris's hair, and William had retreated to the mouth of the Home Tree to pull down his sleeves and wipe his eyes.

Before he could speak, an excited "Dani! Dani!" erupted behind him, and Aeris turned just in time for Hori to swoop down onto his shoulder and hook a wing around his neck for balance. A flurry of giggles followed him, and Aeris called up a *see-by-night* for stronger sight in the dark.

Sen led a small parade of her siblings up to Aeris, both of her clawed hands cupped over her mouth. Bri, just behind her, reached up with two of her pincered hands to tug on the knee of Aeris's trousers.

"Sen's gonna say something!" she announced. "You gotta get close!"

Aeris crouched as bidden. As soon as he was at eye-level, Sen dropped her hands and coughed out a "Hello!" that was lost in a hailstorm of laughter as a crowd of wild-lights burst out of her mouth like a flurry of sparks. One caught against her canines before it drifted out, and Aeris could see, in its flickering light, twin slivers of new teeth, white and flat, where two more of her fangs had fallen out.

"Sen!" He rocked back on his heels in playful surprise. "*Where* did you find so many of those?"

She bounced on her toes, her laugh a cackle. "It's twelve!" she cried. "I got twelve!"

"It was thirteen, but she swallowed one!"

William made an involuntary, concerned noise behind him, and twelve pairs of eyes across seven children flicked in his direction.

"Oh!" Sen's serrated grin flared wider. "Is he sleeping here now?"

Aeris glanced over his unoccupied shoulder at their guest. William's bitten lower lip and the uncertain rise of his shoulders served as answer enough. "Not this time, sweetling," Aeris replied, turning back to Sen. "But I am afraid it *is* nearly bedtime. Please tell the others they may have one last game, and then we will go inside."

At *inside*, the children scattered, all except Hori who pushed his nose against Aeris's ear. "I'll tell 'em, Dani," he promised and added, to William, "You're okay when you're not a ghost." With a skate of his claws against Aeris's shirt, he launched himself into the air and vanished.

"Do I need to sleep here?" William asked, audibly uneasy, as Aeris rose. "I mean, eventually, but-- Do you need me to stay here?"

"Not yet, no. Not if you do not want to."

The *shh* of William's steps in the grass, the barest brush of a hand against his elbow. "How much time do you have?" he asked, his voice as soft as his touch.

"I could not say." The midnight hiccup of the heartbeat against his palm, the rictus of his cheek against the pads of his fingers. Aeris shrugged, as much to shake off the lingering sensation as to suggest uncertainty. "Enough, I think."

A breeze rustled through the forest's branches and stirred up skittering piles of dead leaves. Nothing flickered in the shadows beyond the border, but Aeris couldn't help the prickle of apprehension that settled on the back of his neck.

"Did anything meet you in the Woods?" he asked, and though the question should not have been asked lightly, he asked it so, with a tilt to his head to further belie the sobriety of it.

"No? Was something supposed to?"

"No."

"Then that's kind of a creepy question."

He could not walk William home, not with his children awake and scattered. So he shifted Mika to one arm and unhooked one of his earrings. This he held out to William, who, upon seeing it, took an uncertain step back.

"I don't really-- I don't wear those anymore."

"You need not wear it. Carry it with you."

"Why?"

"As a ward."

"A ward against what?"

"Against creatures not so charming as I."

William shot him a disbelieving frown but did (if reluctantly) hold out his hand. Aeris dropped the earring onto his palm, and William cupped his other hand over it as if he held a live centipede instead of jewelry.

"You will be safe," Aeris promised, and before William could move away, he put his hand on William's, the earring overlaid by two hands instead of one. *"Stay-sharp."*

"Why?" William asked, apparently oblivious to the magic seeping into his skin. "So I can stab them with it?"

Aeris favored him with the same crooked smile he'd seen playing at the corner of William's mouth. "So that it comes back such that I can wear it again."

"Ah." That earned a flicker of the sought-after smile. "Then I guess I'll see you again soon."

XI

AN ITCH—a scratch—a searing heat--

Aeris snapped awake, bristling with fangs and fur and venom enough to kill. He twisted out of the Home Tree—quick and cold, a knife in the dark—and skidded into the leaves, claws out, at the edge of the clearing.

The Tall Ones laughed and flickered, their amusement an incandescence in their skin. With the uncertain dark of midnight as a shroud, they might have been ghosts or wights or fallen stars. They wavered at the border, thin and stretched-out, their skin a pale, sickly near-purple.

"Do you think it wise, Aeris?" one asked. "To bring another kit into your den?"

"Go away." Aeris deepened his voice to a rumble. Venom pulsed, white-hot, against the inside of his cheek. "Go *away*."

Bright and fearless, they laughed again. The one who had spoken before smiled, and his teeth were jagged. "What do you want him for, Aeris? He is not an infant. He is not a child."

"He is not for the taking."

"He is human—and alive—and we want him." The speaker's mouth twisted into a sneer. "For now, you shield him, but we can wait. We will catch him."

"You will *not* touch him."

Another laugh, this one hard and sharp. "Your magic is small, princeling. How quickly might you burn through what is left?" As one, the speaker and the others drifted forward, and Aeris dug his heels into the earth, fought the panic that curdled in the pit of his stomach.

"Go *away*," he growled again, but the Tall Ones crouched and slid fallen leaves away from the line of the barrier. The thin white roots of their fingers wormed into the dirt and sent heat skittering beneath Aeris's skin. He could feel them prying at the border, hunting sightless for any seam or crack or fissure.

Cold near-winter wind lashed at Aeris's fur and the low cut of his ears. This was a sanctuary—this was *home*—and they would not take it. *Go away* snagged on his tongue, but they would come back, and they would come back, and they would come back, and—soon, too soon—Aeris would not be there to push them away.

Grow. His claws sank into the grass and leaves. *Grow.*

The Tall Ones snatched their hands back as thorns and snarled branches erupted at their feet. Brambles curled up out of the earth, sloughing off dirt and dead leaves as they rose, twisting and writhing, first between Aeris and his attackers, then down the line of the boundary. In an arc Aeris felt more than saw, the new growth swept along the edge of the clearing, surged up from the earth in a wild, tangled mess.

Grow.

Branches arched and spiraled higher, sprouted new needle-sharp thorns and clusters of pointed leaves. The Tall Ones stepped back. Pearlescent drops of blood beaded their fingers. They watched, as Aeris did, as the brambles rose waist-high and then stilled.

"Stay *out.*" Exhaustion slammed into Aeris like a fist, and his legs trembled as energy leeched out of him into the earth, but still he held his ground. "Stay *away.*"

One of the Tall Ones wiped her hand against her cheek, leaving a smear of silver blood along her jaw. "The forest spat you out," she hissed, "and it will swallow you up."

"Not yet." This was his home and his family and his heart, and the Tall Ones were welcome to none of it. "Not tonight."

"Once you are dead, your patch of weeds will not keep us out."

Aeris did not answer—he did not have the energy to answer—but the Tall Ones did not wait for a reply. They drifted out of focus, as indistinct as if seen through fog, and when Aeris next blinked, they were gone. Their spearmint stink faded, too, until Aeris could smell only earth and grass and decay.

Unseen, then, at least for now, he dropped his wild shape and sank into the grass. He wanted to sleep, wanted *so dearly* to sleep, and only the burning in his hands and in the soles of his feet kept him awake. His arms and legs ached, and even lying in the grass, he could not stop their trembling. What had the brambles pulled out of him if this was the cost of their invocation?

Stay awake.

Aeris knew better, but he closed his eyes. He was so tired. He could sleep here, just for a moment. He could sink into the grass, into the earth, and cocoon himself in the settling dark. No harm would come from a short rest.

A flutter—a flicker of thought. Dawn might still have been hours off, but someone in the Home Tree drifted toward wakefulness. He could feel them stirring, could feel the slow resolution of their awareness. Aimee: awake now, properly so, as she sought Aeris and found him missing.

Not this. Not yet. Stay awake.

With a heavy exhale, Aeris pushed himself upright. His heart hitched in his throat, but he straightened, palms and soles still burning, and limped back to the Home Tree. Partway there, another wave of exhaustion washed over him, and he curled in on himself, entered the Tree in the smallest and least-taxing shape he could.

Despite the altercation outside, everyone in the Tree still slept—all except Aimee, who swiveled her ears in Aeris's direction as he padded inside. She turned toward him, whiskers twitching. She recognized him, if not by shape then by scent, and that alone settled her: she rolled over and burrowed back beneath her blanket.

Aeris, kitten-shaped, wobbled on short legs to his own bed. He clawed his way onto the pile of blankets and curled up on his own pillow with his nose tucked into his paws. *This* sort of sleep was a thin substitute, a half-hearted dip beneath the surface of a lake fathoms-deep, but it would serve. For now, it would serve.

XII

"YOU'RE JUST MAKING KNOTS."

"You have to tie them in, or they fall out."

"You're doing it wrong. You're supposed to braid them in."

"No, you have to tie 'em."

Aeris blinked, his vision and thoughts blurred by sleep. While his hands and feet still burned, the pain had quieted to a distant ache. He wriggled one hand, found human fingers instead of paws, and let out a long, long sigh of relief.

Tiny claws tugged at his hair, too gently to have woken him, and the culprits continued to whisper as if they thought Aeris still asleep:

"That's just *knots.*"

"Yeah, to keep 'em in." Even Sorrel's whisper was rough stone. "I already told you."

84

"But you're doing it *wrong*," and Aeris recognized that one as Hori, his voice just shy of a panicked squeak. "Let me do it."

"You can't. You don't have fingers."

With an exaggerated yawn, Aeris stretched his arms above his head and pretended not to hear the flurry of "Shh—Shh—*Shhh*!" at his back. He slowly pushed himself upright (to a gasp and muffled giggles), began to brush a hand through his hair, and paused with a "Hmm?" as his fingers caught at the first of Sorrel's knots.

"What's this?" he asked, falsely innocent, and the giggles at once spilled over into outright laughter and nearly drowned Hori's desperate, "I tried to tell her, Dani! I *tried*!"

Aeris slid what felt like a twig from the depths of his hair and held it up for a closer inspection. This time, thankfully, the object in question truly was a stick rather than something alive and displeased.

"'Sweetling, 'tis alright." He favored first Hori, then Sorrel with an indulgent smile. "This is lovely work."

"We wanted to do flowers, but there aren't any left," Sorrel explained, as Aeris pulled the long, loose curtain of his hair over his shoulder to see what else had been tangled into it. "And I tied them in there real tight, so they'd stay."

He found more twigs, sharp-scented pine needles, dead leaves that disintegrated at a touch. A mushroom sported several clumsy knots along its stalk, the frothy gold cap of it softly bright against the smooth oil-black of his hair.

"Yes, these will stay in *very* well." He crumbled one of the dead leaves and brushed the residue from his fingertips. "The trouble might be in taking them out."

"Taking them *out*?"

"Yes, love. With knots like this, if anyone pulls on the ornaments in my hair, I will be hurt. If you help me untie these, we can try something less dangerous."

Sorrel wrinkled her nose at that, but Hori crawled into Aeris's lap without further prompting and combed a claw through what strands he could reach. At Aeris's soft, "Thank you, sweetling," Sorrel relented and clambered onto Aeris's knee to help.

Between the three of them, only Aeris could really untie the knots. Sorrel's bony fingers made precision difficult, and Hori had only the single hooks on the ends of his wings. Aeris unraveled the mess with a patient slowness and tried not to wince as one or the other of his helpers pulled too hard at a stubborn tangle.

He could hear the usual stir of morning activity outside: sleepy, indistinct chatter from those still drowsy; the clap-and-pat of hands in a rhythm game; Mika's gurgling laughter; and, with more enthusiasm than skill, a small contingent singing loud and off-key:

"I have a hat, a hat, a hat!
It's on my head, my head, my head!
I wear a hat, a hat, a hat!
I throw it off, off, off,
And now it's gone, gone, gone!"

A cheer went up, even from those not singing, and then the next verse began (*"I have a shoe, a shoe, a shoe..."*), the words eclipsed by an occasional "My hand's gotten stuck," from Sorrel or "Can I eat this?" from Hori.

This was supposed to last forever. Aeris tried to push the thought away, but as he gently untangled Sorrel's spiked knuckles from the strands of a knot, the sentiment circled back, as implacable as the tide: these mornings, this innocence—this was supposed to last forever.

A droplet struck the edge of his thumb and trickled, cold and narrow, down his wrist. Aeris touched his cheek and found it damp, and realized he was crying in the same moment that Hori looked up at him, likewise startled.

"Dani?"

"Never you mind, love." Aeris touched his cheek again, tempted both to feign indifference and to rub away the evidence as quickly as possible. "I may have caught something in my eye."

Hori looked doubtful, his ears flat, but Sorrel began to pick through the refuse of what had been in Aeris's hair. "But these are all big things," she said, cracking a pinecone beneath the ridge of her thumb. Then, seeing the small and splintered pieces, she hesitated, seemed to reconsider, and began to gather all the discarded oddments into her arms. "These are dangerous now," she announced, matter-of-fact. "I'm going to take them outside."

"Thank you, sweetling." *Steady, steady, steady.* "You may both play outside if you like. I can manage the rest."

Sorrel wobbled to her feet and, blithe and overloaded, marched out of the Tree. As Hori watched her go, Aeris swept unseen at what remained of his tears. By the time Hori turned back to him, Aeris could blink down at him, dry-eyed and very, very still.

"Go play," he insisted, even as Hori made no move to follow his sibling. "Go on."

"You don't like it when *we* do that, Dani."

"Do what, darling?"

"When we hide that we're sad."

I am not sad, he wanted to protest, but with another blink, Aeris found that a lie. He wiped at his cheek again, his palm damp, and set his jaw against an honest reply. "Do you think I am hiding so?" he asked, but even without the snag in his voice, the attempt at deflection was a clumsy one.

"Yes," Hori replied. In another mood, Aeris would have laughed upon hearing such fierce certitude from one so small. "Why are you crying?"

What could he give but the truth—or a facet of it? "I was thinking," he began, slowly, his eyes on his hands, "of how dearly beloved a place this is, and how all of you make it so."

"Oh." Hori flicked his ears but did not lift them, and the fur along his shoulders began to settle. He did not seem to know quite what to do with Aeris's answer, and he tilted his head in a gesture Aeris recognized as his own.

In the pause, Aeris drew in as quiet a calming breath as he could. Sorrow would not be allowed to grow here; he pushed it away and—throat tight, chest tight—buried it deep, froze it in winter's dead, frigid soil. No sorrow, no tears, no remorse at all.

"One does not have to be sad to cry," he went on, his new cheer too bright, too fast. "Think nothing of it, little one."

"Why are you thinking that today?" Hori asked, in a far more uncertain tone than Aeris had expected, and Aeris tensed to hear it. "Is it because of Sen?"

"Sen?"

"Her teeth are falling out." Hori hooked his claws together, hunched his shoulders up toward the sharp line of his jaw. "That means she's going to leave soon."

89

Ah. Aeris relaxed in the face of this familiar concern, the softening of his mien and voice so habitual as to be instinctive. "Yes, love. She is molting."

"I don't want to do that."

"You shall not, love. Not if you do not want to."

Hori tucked himself smaller. "Is it bad? If I don't ever want to?"

With the child already in his lap, Aeris had only to lean forward, arms open, to draw Hori into a hug so tight that Hori squeaked in surprise. "My dear, how could such a thing be bad?" He pressed a kiss to the top of Hori's just-visible head. For all that he had spoken such reassurances before, the words as well-worn as an old coat, he stitched them anew: "I want you to wear what shape gives you joy and comfort—and if you are so now, how could I think you ought to change?"

"But what if everyone else does?" Hori burrowed against his chest, his voice nearly inaudible. "What if they all change, and I'm the only one who doesn't?"

"Then you stay as you are. Simply that, love: you stay as you are. You stay as long as you like, however you like."

Hori did not respond, and Aeris did not push. He listened, in some measure, to the distant melody of a new verse outside ("*I have a belt, a belt, a belt...*"), but mostly he listened to the susurration of Hori's breath, to the steady ebb and flow of his own, to the little catch in Hori's that preceded his reply:

"I don't want to go back."

Another kiss, this one left on the soft fur between Hori's ears. "You never have to go back, love. I will not send you away."

"You promise?"

"I promise. I shall push you nowhere you are not ready to go." Instead of another kiss, Aeris pushed his nose against Hori's forehead, nuzzled him insistently enough to prompt a reluctant giggle. "Nowhere—except, perhaps, a bath."

That won a second giggle, and after a moment, Hori nodded against Aeris's chest. "Okay." He squirmed in Aeris's embrace, twisted to look up at him, one ear upright and the other flat against Aeris's shirt. "I think I'd like to go sing now."

"Yes, love."

"You come, too."

"Yes, love." Aeris allowed Hori to climb onto his shoulder. "And we shall see if your sibling truly wants to learn to braid, or if her interest lies only in making knots."

"It's the knots."

"Yes, I rather think so, too."

91

XIII

SIXTEEN. Sixteen teeth as smooth and sharp as knives, as white as polished ivory. Sen had begun to lose them in earnest over the last two days, first one by one, then in pairs, each one salvaged and brought at a run to Aeris. Cross-legged, now, in the mouth of the Home Tree, Aeris arranged them in a line along his calf and conjured twin spools of black thread and silver wire. With thumb and forefinger, he pinched off strands of wire and began, one by one, to loop each tooth into a slender metal sling.

Fold and twist. Fold and twist. He pricked his finger on one of the sharper teeth and paused only long enough to hold the wound against his coat until the cut closed on its own. The wire bent easily in his hands, as effortless to work with as wet clay, but the teeth, far more weapon than trinket, did not submit so well.

A mild southern breeze ruffled his hair and his sleeves. The sliver of rising sun lifted the morning dew into a mist, melted the clearing and the wall of thorns and the forest beyond into soft shapes and diaphanous gold. Aeris could hear autumn birdsong from deeper in the Woods, their music muted and faraway.

In this near-silence, he heard William's approach long before he saw him, the rhythmic *shh-shh* of his shoes through the leaves not yet familiar but nearly so. By the time the young man reached the edge of the clearing, Aeris had already opened a path for him between the brambles: a space wide enough only for one, the thorns twisted inward so they would not catch on William's clothes or his skin.

As William passed through the gap, he paid the plants no mind, nor did he seem to notice them relacing behind him. He wore his orange sweatshirt, its color as dusty as an old pumpkin, but neither hat nor coat. Morning mist wreathed his legs; the sunlight turned him to smudged gold; and Aeris felt, for the first time in two days, as if he could breathe again.

"Hey," William began as he drew nearer. "How's your morning?"

"All the better for your company." Aeris set the last twist of silver in his lap and regarded him with a cordial smile. "No winter coat yet, I see."

William came to a stop an arm's length away, one shoulder hitched high and his hands stuffed, as usual, into his pockets. He nearly returned the smile (Aeris could see it flicker at the corner of his mouth), but it did not survive longer than a moment. "Don't need one today."

"Did you meet with any trouble?"

"Not from anything spooky, no." With an easy shrug, William withdrew a small, clear packet from his pocket and held it out for Aeris to take. "Here's this for you."

The plastic bag contained, on inspection, Aeris's gifted earring. Aeris tipped it out onto his hand and let it settle in the crease of his palm. Silver and sharp and returned, as promised, such that he could wear it again.

Aeris raised it in open-handed offer. "I would see you keep this, even if you do not wear it."

"I'm grateful for the offer, but..." William trailed off with another shrug, this one less casual. "I just... felt like I shouldn't have it."

"You know," Aeris began, tilting his head to more easily replace the hook in his ear, "I do not expect recompense for a gift. You could keep the coat or the earring without obligation."

"It's not that, it's--" William broke off and hiked his other shoulder up to join the first. He hesitated, flushed either with cold or with embarrassment, before mustering the rest of his reply: "I can't wear it, and I don't want to lose it or... or have someone ask me why I have it. I-- I guess-- I'm uncomfortable—having it makes me uncomfortable."

"And the coat?"

"I don't own anything that fancy." Here, at least, William managed a smile, if a self-deprecating one. "Everyone would think I stole it."

"I see." No earrings, then, and nothing made of velvet or lace. "Then I shall not insist."

"You're not mad?"

"Mad?" Aeris leaned back, the question too unexpected for him to hide his surprise. "Of course not. Why would I be so?"

"I don't know. It's just... you keep giving me things, and I keep giving them back."

"There is nothing in that for me to be mad about; it signifies that my gifts do not suit. You ought to be warm and safe, but not at the expense of your peace of mind."

"Oh." William took his turn to look startled. "I-- Are you sure?"

"Quite so. If I were displeased, I would tell you."

Another hesitation, this one marked by a restless shift from one foot to the other, and then, without speaking further, William joined him in the mouth of the Home Tree. Aeris could not reposition himself, not with his work balanced so carefully on his lap, but neither was he inclined to move as his guest sat beside him, close enough this time for his shoulder to knock against Aeris's as he settled into place.

"What are you working on? Are those shark teeth?"

Aeris did not comment on the blatant change of subject, only picked up one of the teeth and passed it to William for closer inspection. "They are Sen's baby teeth, so to speak."

"Really?" William held the tooth up against the still-rising sun. "They're *huge*."

"She wants them as a necklace."

"She wants to *wear* these?"

"Yes." Aeris turned a fond smile from the teeth to William. "She was quite insistent."

"Damn." There, at last: the start of a genuine grin. William's smiles seemed to be crooked, all on one side and not the other, but laughter lit his eyes and his voice as he replied, amused but earnest, "I *really* like your family."

Pride and delight filled, in a dizzying rush, the cavity of his chest, and Aeris could not help but laugh. "I am most pleased to hear it," he replied, turning deliberately away from William's widening smile. He swept the rest of the teeth into his hands, the *click* and *tap* of one against the other almost like music. "Hold these if you would. Mind the edges."

Still smiling, William pulled on the bottom hem of his sweatshirt to produce a makeshift bowl, and Aeris tipped the handful in with a soft clatter. While William watched, Aeris took the spool of black string and unwound enough for a necklace. He paused, then, reconsidering, and altered the thread to cord tough enough to withstand Sen's roughhousing. That done, he severed the length from the whole and turned up his hand for the first of the teeth. As William set one upon his palm, he slid it onto the end of the cord and held out his hand for the next one.

"Are you worried she might cut herself on something like this?" William asked as he passed over the next tooth. "It's like wearing a string of knives."

"A little, perhaps, but I suspect blunting them would likewise blunt the appeal."

Another tooth passed over, another *click* as it slid onto the cord to join the rest. "Have you done this before? Made jewelry out of your kids' teeth, I mean."

"No, Sen's necklace will be the first," Aeris answered, all sobriety, then added, teasing, "Why, did you want one made from your own?"

97

"Ah, well, I didn't save any of my baby teeth. What a shame."

"A shame indeed." Aeris cast William a sideways glance, found him smiling still, and failed to resist doing the same. "I am beginning to suspect, dear William, that your calling me trouble was of a piece with the pot and the kettle."

William laughed, but did not riposte, and the only sound between them, then, was the *click* of each new tooth knocking against those already strung.

Working with deliberate slowness, they managed to stretch the task through what remained of the dawn. As the sun rose, bands of sunlight stretched between the trees, turned their leaves lantern-bright, green and autumn crimson. Aeris could feel his family beginning to wake, could feel the earlier risers stretching and swimming against the tides of sleep.

Sen's wakefulness crackled like an electric bolt through Aeris's mind, and just as he finished the sliding knot on her necklace, she launched herself at his back and squirmed her way under his arm to fling herself into his lap.

"Is it ready?" she asked, barely managing a whisper, and threw her hands up in silent glee when Aeris held the necklace up for her inspection. Without even waiting for him to let go, she grabbed his hands and pulled the necklace down around her head.

"Keep still for a moment, love." Aeris pulled the cord free from her ears and adjusted the knot at the back of her neck. "What do you think?"

"This is my most favorite thing I've ever had," Sen announced, her voice hitching into a squeak, "and I'm never ever *ever* taking it off!"

"Do you hear that, William? We did excellent work."

William, as Aeris turned to look at him, nodded—serious, now, and newly awkward. With his hands clasped in his lap, he skated the pad of his thumb over the ruined skin of his knuckles.

Aeris hooked his hands beneath Sen's arms. "Do you remember William?" he asked, swinging her easily up into the air.

Sen giggled and kicked her dangling legs. As an answer, she twisted as best she could in William's direction and peeled down the corners of her mouth to show off what teeth she had left. William, unsmiling, did the same, pulling down his lower lip in an exaggerated grimace.

"Perfect." Aeris placed Sen at his hip and, with his two companions making faces at each other, pushed himself to his feet. "Amuse each other thus while I check on those still waking."

Sen garbled an "M'kay," and so Aeris withdrew into the Tree, half his mind on the pair behind him. William might have been nervous, anxious to please and to cause no harm, but he would learn for himself that his children were not made of glass.

Inside the Tree, wild-lights flickered out of sight as the sun stole over their glow. Someone yawned; someone else mumbled a drowsy protest against the morning. The air felt thick with sleep, slow and peaceful, and Aeris padded soundlessly along the Tree's inner curve. He checked each hollow as he went, straightening blankets, untangling one from around Poe's horns and pulling another over Ann's hind legs. He heard Mika fussing before he reached him, and he found Aimee trying to soothe him, one paw patting uncertainly at the baby's forehead.

"How are we this morning?" he asked, crouching beside the pair.

"I'm still tired." Aimee's giant brown eyes met his. "And Mika work up squirmy."

Mika whined. As Aeris leaned forward to peer at him, the he raised his arms, grasping at nothing with his doughy fingers. Aeris picked him up, and the whining subsided; as Aeris settled Mika against his chest, the baby squashed his cheek against Aeris's shoulder and closed one hand against the velvet of his coat.

"You may go back to sleep, Aimee, if you are still tired."

With a drowsy nod, Aimee curled up in the hollow left by Mika's absence. "I want to sleep all day," she mumbled, burrowing her nose into her paws.

"Then sleep well, love." Aeris, one-handed, eased her blanket up to her whiskers, then renewed his hold on Mika and rose.

He returned to the entrance to find Amaya awake with William and Sen; Pel perched on one of the roots just outside, his carapace whorled with rainbow hues in the newly-risen sun. William glanced up as Aeris drew near, and the upward creep of his shoulders abated. No longer making faces at Sen, he had folded his hands in his lap again, one thumb in a dangerous back-and-forth across the back of his other hand.

"Look at my necklace!" Sen insisted, hindered in her presentation by her refusal to take it off. "Look at my teeth!"

"We've seen your teeth," Pel replied. "We saw 'em when they were in your mouth."

"Yeah, but now you can see 'em *better*."

Aeris abandoned his original place in the threshold to sit against the Tree's inner curve, close enough to William to return the earlier nudge against his shoulder. William did not retreat, but neither did he look again at Aeris or still his hands.

"They're so *sharp*," Amaya whispered. "You could use them to cut stuff up."

Sen remained silent for a moment, apparently considering this. "No," she answered eventually, her voice thoughtful rather than defiant. "I just want to wear them."

William dug the short nail of his thumb into his ill-healing cuts, and Aeris pushed his shoulder against his guest's. "None of that," he murmured, then added, more gently still as he saw William's ears turn pink, "I will not see you hurt yourself."

He was tempted to seize William's hand, too, if necessary, but William desisted at once. He nodded, his blush stealing over the rest of his face, and left his hands as fists on his knees.

Gradually, other children woke and wandered closer. Bess fluttered from her alcove to land beside Pel and began the morning work of resettling her feathers. Finn crawled into Aeris's lap and stuck his nose into one of his coat's inner pockets. Hori flapped over and hung upside-down from the upper curve of the Tree's doorway. Sen, of course, addressed each new arrival, and their collective exclamations grew louder and more frequent:

"Look! Look what Dani made for me!"

"Whooooa, they look so sharp!"

"What happens when you lose more of them? Can you stick 'em on?"

"Does it make noise? Make it make noise!"

As Sen rattled her necklace, June drifted over to the group. Her gaze caught at once on William, as his did on her, and she darted around Aeris's legs to reach him.

"Good morning--" William began, but June slid under his arm to sit in his lap, and as he raised his hands, not sure what to do with them, she grabbed one and turned it over to inspect his knuckles. Aeris watched William's hand tense in hers, watched him study the moss and flowers growing in the cracks of her skin even as she investigated his.

But after only a moment's inspection, she tilted her head back and turned sad, silver eyes up to his. "Yours aren't getting better," she whispered, and Aeris could hear the shiver of confusion and heartbreak in her voice.

William heard it, too; he softened, his hands loose and his shoulders low, and he leaned to one side to better see and talk to her. "They're alright, they're just healing slowly," he replied, as mild as summer. "It's taking so long because I keep picking at them."

"Why do you do that?"

"It's a bad habit." Though Sen and the others were laughing at the racket made by Sen's necklace, William didn't seem to hear. "I'm sorry if seeing them like this bothers you."

"Do they hurt?"

"Not much, no."

June's frown waned, but only partially. She dropped her chin and resumed her perusal, one fingertip tracing the reddened edges of his cuts. "Are they going to grow flowers?"

"No, I don't think so."

"They might if you eat the fruit."

"The fruit?" William asked, confused, and shot a glance at Aeris. "What fruit?"

"Everyone gets one," June explained, but that, of course, was only a sliver of the truth, and Aeris supplied the rest:

"To eat is to accept sanctuary—to stay." William blinked at that, newly focused, but did not interrupt. "What grows on the Tree abates the hunger of the one who eats, and they need no mortal food. And while they live in the Wild, the Wild seeps in. From such borrowed magic grow the fangs and scales and such Wild raiments as my children so desire."

"Did you eat some of it, too?" William asked, as June began to play with his fingers, bending and unbending his thumb. "Is that why you can turn into animals?"

"No. I did not need to eat. I am a being of the Woods, and I was born as I am."

"But there's enough? For everyone who wants to stay?"

"Yeah, there's always enough," June put in, now squashing William's index and middle fingers together. "Everybody gets one."

"So do I--" William broke off, and Aeris's heart twisted to hear the longing in his voice. The young man's blush, previously abated, returned in full, and William kept his eyes on his knees, his expression wistful and hungry and embarrassed by both. "Do I have one, too?"

Aeris drew in a breath to answer, then realized he didn't know. William was not a lost child, not like Sen or Hori or any of the others. Would something grow? *Could* something grow? Mika's portion had been so much smaller than those before; what if that had been the last?

"I bet he's got one." This from Finn, who had finally removed his nose from Aeris's pocket. "Can we check, Dani?"

"Check what?" Pel asked, and with his attention came that of the rest of those awake.

Aeris, for the moment, did not answer either question, nor did he acknowledge the influx of observers. He kept his eyes on William, even as William avoided his. "You are in earnest, then?" he asked, too softly for his voice to betray any of his own curiosity. "You want to stay?"

Without looking up, William nodded once. June continued to push and pull the fingers of one hand, and he rested the other on his knee, first as a fist, then flat, then as a fist again.

"Then, Bess, if you would, please."

With a squawk, Bess took off from her perch and disappeared out of sight. Aeris tried not to guess at what she might find, but he could think of nothing else. What if Bess came back with nothing? Would William look on that as a bad omen? William did not need to eat from the Tree to stay, but, in the absence of such an endorsement, would he still want to?

None of them waited long. Within a few seconds, Bess returned with a rustle of feathers. "There was one growing," she announced, before anyone could ask. She opened one claw to tumble the fruit into Aeris's palm, and Aeris froze.

It might have been a seed, wet with morning dew, had it not been lopsided and scarlet, unmistakable in color and shape. A handful of short, bristling stems grew twisted from the upper half, and the presence of it left a slight (very slight) warmth against his skin. An errant breath would have blown it from Aeris's hand.

Embarrassment and shame rose hot and prickling up his spine and left him queasy. He could not give this to William. This was a gift worth nothing in the giving. Such a small and pathetic thing could not sustain William properly, nor could the offering of it be seen as anything but a shallow gesture of inclusion.

A bump against his shoulder jolted him back into the present. The children clustered around him to peer at the fruit, and William leaned flush against him to do the same, his cheek nearly brushing Mika's brown hair.

"Is that it?" Amaya asked, her nose so close to the fruit that Aeris was briefly afraid it would disappear inside. "It's even smaller than Mika's."

"Maybe it's 'cause he's a grown-up," Pel suggested. "Grown-ups barely eat anything."

"Grown-ups eat more than anybody! They have all that extra inside space they have to fill up."

"But a kid's inside space is all for food. Grown-ups have to leave space for other stuff. Like math and remembering the laundry."

While his children bickered, Aeris's gaze slid to William, and he found the young man looking not at the fruit but at him, his own uncertainty reflected in the slope of William's mouth and the furrow between his eyebrows.

He had to give it. Mortified both by the possibility of William accepting such a pitiful gift and of his refusing it, Aeris reached around Mika to present the tiny offering. "You need not eat it now," he insisted, as William trapped the fruit between two fingers, "nor is it a requisite, if you wish to stay."

William inspected it first with one eye closed, then the other. He glanced at Aeris again, his expression unchanged. He wanted a cue, some suggestion of how to react, but Aeris did not know in which direction to prompt him.

"They're not always this little?" William asked, and with Aeris so near, he did not need to lift his voice above a bare whisper.

The young man's unwavering green-and-brown gaze felt less, this time, like a stake through his chest, but unease seeped cold into Aeris's bones nonetheless. The question hung unasked between them: *Is this by chance, or is this because the Tree is sick?*

"I am afraid," he admitted at last, so faintly that his voice might have been drowned by the children's argument brewing around them, "that you would still be hungry."

For the space of one long breath, William did not move. Then he exhaled and, as decisive as if he had not considered any other course, freed his hand from June's, picked up the plastic bag he had brought the earring in, and dropped the fruit inside.

Amaya's attention caught at the movement. "You're not eating it?" she asked, curiosity in her voice and in the rise of her ears. "Why're you putting it away?"

"I'm saving it for later," William answered, full of a conviction Aeris did not understand.

"How come?"

Before he answered, William set the bag against the edge of the threshold, where it was least likely to be stepped on, then let June reclaim his hand. "Because," he began, "I want to make sure I use it the right way."

"You eat it, that's the way."

Sen spoke up from her place at Amaya's shoulder: "If you wait, it'll get squishy."

"It's already squishy."

"That's true." Satisfied by this logic, Sen let the matter drop. "Play catch with us."

"Play--? Oh." William glanced, as before, at Aeris for guidance, and Aeris, as before, did not know how to direct him. The young man hunched his shoulders, as if reluctant to go, but as much as Aeris wanted likewise to talk, to ask what William meant by keeping the fruit, they could not speak here, not in the midst of so many attentive ears.

So Aeris offered a rueful smile. "There is time. Go on."

With a nod, William turned back to Sen and Amaya, who had begun to chew on the hem of his jeans. "Okay. Play catch with what?"

Bess squawked a laugh. "With us, silly!"

"Like... I'm going to toss you?"

"No! Like this!" Sen darted forward and smacked a hand against William's knee. "Caught you! Now catch us!"

All the children, even June and Finn, scattered like dropped marbles. As fast as instinct, like a hound tearing after rabbits, William surged to his feet and shot after them. Shrieks of laughter and "Catch him—catch *him*!" filled the clearing like raucous birdsong.

Even with the advantage of longer legs, William spent more time chasing than being chased. Each time he caught up to one of the children, he would falter and draw back, and the nearly-caught would slip out of reach like a fish in a pond. Sen eventually took pity on him: Aeris watched her trot up to William and point at her head, shoulders, and hands, her mouth moving with words Aeris could not hear. Then she held out her hand, which William tapped with his own, and she raced after the nearest of her siblings.

The gauntlet passed, then, from Sen to Hori to Finn to Amaya. When it looped back to William, he caught Sen with a hand atop her head, pausing just long enough to ruffle her hair and send her into a fit of giggles. On every turn after, he did much the same, disheveling hair or fur or feathers when he could, touching two fingers to a shoulder when he could not.

Aeris set his back against the Tree and resettled Mika against his chest. The infant's breath fluttered warm against his neck with each sleepy exhale. Aeris closed his eyes for a moment and drank in the morning—his children happy, his arms full, the future unknown but hopeful—until his heart was saturated with it. If he could not hold onto all this forever, he could at least keep the memory, could fold it like a pressed flower into the deepest pocket of his thoughts.

One by one, those still in the Tree woke and wandered into the morning light. Mira and Orion sat with Aeris for a spell, groggy and slow to rub the sleep out of their eyes, but most bristled with energy as they scrambled outside to join the ongoing game. Only Eris woke and hung back, the blue glow of his mushrooms all that was visible of him beneath the trailing ends of Aeris's coat.

The shadows shrank as the sun rose toward noon, and finally William staggered back to the Tree and dropped, exhausted, beside Aeris. He tipped onto his back, arms outstretched, and Aeris tilted sideways to peer down at him.

"How do you fare?" he asked, and then, when William answered with a laugh all air and no sound, asked instead, "Do you need a rest?"

"Just for a minute. I haven't... I haven't run this much since high school."

"At a glance, it would seem you have missed it."

William met his eyes with a sunburst of a smile, and Aeris drank him in, too. The cinnamon dust of his freckles, the rosy flush in his cheeks, the wild edge to his grin.

A shout of "*William!*" preceded the smack of Poe against William's shin, and both Aeris and William straightened to find a gathering flock and a flurry of protests:

"You have to keep playing!"

"You can't be tired!"

"Yeah! *We* aren't tired!"

"You don't even have to run; you can just walk and chase us."

William ran a hand through the mess of his hair and struggled valiantly to catch his breath. "Okay," he conceded, to a riot of approval, "but let's do the other kind of catch."

"What's the other kind?" Finn asked, as William slid from the edge of the Tree and back out into the clearing.

"It's when I throw something, and you catch it and throw it back."

"Oh! That's *toss.*"

Despite the profusion of leaves, sticks, and mushrooms, nothing outside the Tree quite suited the purpose, so William took off one of his shoes. He knotted the laces to keep them from trailing

112

and tossed the shoe into a forest of arms. Amaya caught it first and flung it back, and William, stumbling sideways, half barefoot, managed to catch it one-handed. Amidst a clamor of "Back up, back up!" and "Throw it higher, throw it higher!" he obliged, and retreated step by step to the edge of the clearing to throw the makeshift ball as far as he could. Whoever caught the shoe passed it to Pel or Bess, who delivered it to William and returned dragonfly-fast to their siblings in time for the next throw.

The game might have lasted as long as the one previous had William, on one particularly zealous throw, not taken one too many staggering steps back, lost his balance, and crashed headlong into the brambles.

« « « » » »

"Sorry I ruined the day."

"You did nothing of the kind. I am sorry you are hurt."

William dabbed a square of cotton against his jaw and winced as the fabric scraped against his reopened wound; Aeris flinched in sympathy and dug his fingernails into his palms to keep from intervening.

"*Shit,* that stings," William hissed, trying again to minister to his injuries. Amidst the raised scarlet scratches the brambles had left across his face, they had also cracked open the cut on his cheek. Blood and sap had mixed into a sticky, viscous mess from temple to jaw and pulled at the pad's fraying cotton.

Behind them, sheltered in the Tree, Mika lay wrapped in Aeris's discarded coat and Eris sat with him, his chin on Mika's rising, falling chest. The rest of the children, though protesting, had allowed Aeris to shoo them away; they retreated only as far as necessary and then crouched to watch, leaving William and Aeris relatively alone at the edge of the clearing.

William winced again, and Aeris drew in a sharp breath. "May I?" he asked, already reaching for the cotton square, and William hesitated only briefly before he passed it over.

"Did we break him?" Sen called from some distance behind them.

"I'm okay!" William called back, as Aeris touched his chin. "Just banged up."

"You promise?"

"I promise!"

Aeris gently tilted William's head to one side and dabbed at the blood beading along his cheek. "I *am* sorry," he said again, stomach twisting as William flinched at the contact. "I should have warned you away from the thorns."

"It's not your fault." William managed a wry twist of a smile. "At least I got as much blood on the plants as they got on me."

Aeris did not answer with more than his own thin attempt at a smile. Despite the tilt to William's mouth, the young man held utterly still and kept his eyes open as Aeris worked. This was William as alley cat, watchful and uneasy, and Aeris cared for nothing, for the moment, save the need for gentleness. He wiped blood and dirt from the scratches, checking as he went for thorns embedded splinter-small in his skin.

But as he touched the cotton to the underside of William's jaw, Aeris paused, fingers and fabric gentle and at rest. "Why did you not eat?" he asked, soft and low and careful to keep his eyes downcast.

As if he had expected the question, William answered at once: "Because it might be the last one." His voice, equally quiet, sounded flat. "If you give it to me, you can't give it to a kid who might need it."

"I *am* giving it to you." Aeris flicked his eyes up, met green and brown and did not blink. "Whether it is the last one or not, it is yours."

William shrugged, affecting disinterest, and Aeris's skin prickled. "You said I don't *need* to eat it, right?"

"I did say so, yes."

115

"Then it would be a waste if I did, wouldn't it? When it could go to someone who can't live here without it?"

Aeris swept bark-like flakes from William's cheek and touched a finger to the scratches to check for continued bleeding. "No," he answered, softer still. "It would not be a waste. Not if you see it as a mark of your right to be here."

"I don't," William replied, too quickly. "I don't see it that way."

Though Aeris felt the lie of that, too, like a pinprick at the back of his neck, he did not argue. He smoothed a smudge of dirt from William's temple and brushed back his hair to check for veiled injuries. At the ministrations, William kept his hands loosely folded in his lap and, with a small sound almost like a sigh, closed his eyes.

Most of the new scratches had already stopped bleeding, the sap and clotting blood forming unorthodox but effective scabs. William's bruising, those from before his first visit, had all but vanished, and the cut on his cheek, though open again, had narrowed, had turned hard and smooth in a way that a mere two days could not account for.

Observing him thus, and from so marginal a distance, Aeris hesitated before he remarked, deliberately casual, "It has been a while since your last visit."

William kept his eyes closed, but a frisson of guilt pinched his eyebrows. "I know, I'm sorry. A coworker called in sick, so I covered a bunch of her shifts."

"By your count, how many days have you been absent here?"

"I don't know. Four? Five?"

"I see. Not quite so much time has passed for us."

"What?" The young man's eyes snapped opened at that. "How long has it been?"

"Half as many days, but as the seasons change, as the stars change, in one direction or another, the gap will widen." Aeris withdrew, lamenting his distance from his coat. "Time will not pass equal between the world and the Woods."

William shot a quick, uneasy glance at the Tree and the children tussling among the roots. "Dani, that's gonna be a problem. Is there a reason you're not freaking out?"

"Yes: I know how to reinstate a balance. Lend me your wrist if you would. Your left."

William did so at once. Plant debris flecked his sleeves, but without a chance to catch himself as he fell, his hands bore no new injuries.

As easily as if tearing paper, Aeris tore a stretch of cloth from the hem of his own shirt. With a strip twice the length of his hand, he pinched one ragged end and ran the length between his thumb and forefinger. As it passed through his fingers, the fabric darkened, turned from cloth to tawny leather—an alteration more glamour than true transformation.

"Does this suit?" he asked, looping the strip twice around William's outstretched wrist. "For this to work, you must not take it off."

William nodded, serious and focused, and so Aeris unhooked his earring once more, stabbed the hook of it through the loose ends of the leather to form a clasp, and shaped the silver into a closed pin. He melted the extraneous silver into beads: solid drops of mercury that could slide and spin along the fastener.

"There," he announced, giving the bracelet one final tug as he let go. "Your anchor. Now I will need to wear something of yours."

"Like what?"

"Anything, in truth, but that which comes from something you often wear will have the most potency."

After a quick self-inspection in which he examined, doubtful, his jeans and sneakers, William patted his sweatshirt and found one end of the hood's drawstring. He pulled the string free, ignoring the hood's awkward contraction against the nape of his neck.

Without prompting, Aeris held out his left wrist, and William folded the length of string in half, rested the midpoint against Aeris's skin, and tucked the two loose ends into the loop. He pulled the loop tight, the string hitching snug around Aeris's wrist, then wrapped the rest of the doubled cord around and around Aeris's wrist until he ran out of string. In lieu of a knot, he wedged the plastic aglets under the strands.

"Will that work?" he asked and gave Aeris's arm a gentle push back toward him.

Aeris inspected his new bracelet. The cord carried a richer, sunnier color than the sweatshirt—not orange but the warm and buttery yellow of marigolds in full bloom. Quite apart from the relief of ensuring a matched passage of time, he found the tightness of the cord to be a comfort of its own, and he rather liked the bright streak of it against his skin.

"It will. Now give me your hand if you would be so kind."

William held out his hand, again without protest, and Aeris took it, threaded his fingers through William's, joined their hands, left and left. Though William startled at the deliberate contact, he did not withdraw, and, tentative, he curled his fingers over Aeris's knuckles. The warmth of his hand felt like a fire against Aeris's palm, a candle's heat licking harmless but steady against his skin.

"Over the current of my heart's blood, as a band across my wrist, I wear you and carry you with me." The words were not magic, only an explanation of what had already been done, but Aeris's speech slipped into a spell-like smoothness all the same. "With a band I have shaped by my own hand, you carry me with you. With this exchange, thus we are tethered. My time is tied to yours, and yours to mine."

"That's it?" William asked. His fingers tightened, as if in preparation to pull away, but he did not let go.

"Yes." Likewise without letting go, Aeris flashed an arch smile in William's direction. "And you ought to call me Aeris."

"What? Why?"

"'Tis my name."

"Is it?" William blinked, turned his head to study him, almost suspicious, from the corner of one eye. "But your kids call you Dani."

"That is title and endearment." Aeris lifted one shoulder in a gesture of playful nonchalance. "They have never agreed on whether I am mother or father or older sibling, so they gave me a name which is like-but-not all three."

"Oh. So it's like... a family nickname."

"Yes, and though you are part of my family, with you, I would prefer to be Aeris."

"Me, too." William's ears turned rosy, and he abruptly withdrew his hand. "I mean, I haven't thought of *you* as-- as blood-family like that. More like... I dunno." The blush crept down his neck, as pink as the inflamed skin around his newest scratches. "I'd rather call you Aeris."

"Good." Aeris leaned forward and plucked a stray leaf from the tumultuous nest of William's hair, the cord at his wrist nearly gold in the sunlight. "You are to take my place, and that is its own form of kinship."

William's eyes met his briefly, green and brown and inscrutable, before skating away to the black, skeletal branches of the Home Tree. "Yeah," he agreed, as faintly as if he had momentarily forgotten. He fidgeted with the silver pin of his new bracelet, spinning the beads around and around the bar. "Yeah, I guess so."

XIV

RAIN FELL IN SLANTING SHEETS TOO DENSE TO SEE THROUGH, but Aeris kept watch anyway. At the start of the storm, before the gusts and growling thunder, he had seen flashes of moon-bright silver beyond the smudged darkness of the trees. Even if the silver had long since flickered out of sight, Aeris could not loosen the knot of unease in his chest.

Could he fight? If they tore through the wall of thorns, could he push them back? Or would they tear through the thorns and through him and through the Tree?

Wind lashed the bare, distant branches, whipped stinging rain across the mouth of the Tree, but Aeris sheltered safe inside the refuge of the hollow, the rustle of his children asleep a soothing music behind him. Despite the warmth and high collar of his coat, he could feel a near-constant lick of cold against his cheek: a sign, small but unmistakable, of a crack in a once-impenetrable citadel.

So he kept his vigil, his back against the curved wood, his legs stretched across the opening of the Tree. Even weak, even tired, his body could serve as one last barrier between the Tall Ones and his children.

Another gust of wind swept cold against his face, carrying a chill bone-deep and the dense, earth-heavy scent of rain. That scent, the first of his memory, brought with it echoes of the rest: soil thick with rain and rotting wood, the wet tang of iron against the roof of his mouth, dirt cold and clotted against his bare skin.

Ill with nostalgia and nausea both, Aeris turned away from the storm and raised a hand to wipe away the trace of rain on--

William. The smell of him—a whisper of sweat and soap. But, no, William had left before the rain began, was surely, by now, asleep and safe. The scent of him suffused his gifted bracelet, its soft gold a thin, hopeful band of sunlight.

Aeris could picture him easily: tucked into his attic room with no nest but a worn mattress, his mess of blankets a warm and tangled haven from the rain and the wind. He thought, too, of the breathless, wild edges of William's untempered grin, and he realized with a pang that he would miss more than the growth of his own children. William was a clouded spring sky, and Aeris would not live to see him in his summer.

Aeris curled his fingers into the fabric of his shirt and pretended not to notice the coarse grain of his skin or the unyielding stiffness of his knuckles. He could feel his heartbeat as slow and stumbling as the Tree's, a drum halfway out of its proper rhythm.

"Not yet," he whispered, his voice lost in the rattle of falling rain on fallen leaves. He forced his hand flat, set his palm upon his chest, knew his own magic would do nothing even as he pressed *heal heal heal* into his skin. "Not tonight."

His pulse, of course, did not strengthen; the skin under his palm did not soften. Sorrow a stone in his throat, Aeris turned back toward the storm, exhausted and hollow and sick with longing for the sun.

XV

"Cas."

"No! One!"

"Min."

"No! Two!"

"Mira."

That earned mingled cheers and sighs, and Aeris left his eyes closed for a moment longer, listening to the shuffle of Orion trading places with his sister. He could hear them settling, then a pause, then Mira's voice, nearly inaudible: "One... two... three..."

As he listened, sleepy and peaceful, a chitinous arm nudged his own, its owner lifting his elbow just enough to squirm beneath it and settle against his hip. Claws, delicate and serrated, rested against his sleeve; Lily, then, sheltered under his arm. Her chest expanded in the beginning of a deep, contented sigh.

125

"Good morning, little sprout." Aeris tightened his arm around her in lieu of a full-bodied embrace. "How went your night?"

"Good. I had a nice dream. I was eating ice cream in it."

"What flavor of ice cream?"

"Chocolate and strawberry." Lily rested her head against his ribs. "The person at the shop gave it to me because she felt bad that I was by myself. I went and ate it under the flower bushes, and it was so hot outside that it got everywhere."

A memory, then, moreso than a dream. Aeris shifted, wrapped both arms around her to hoist her into his lap. "The bushes with the pink-and-white flowers?" he asked as he tucked her inside his coat. "From the park?"

Lily's antennae brushed his chin as she nodded. "All the bees kept trying to land on me, and I let 'em. And there was a butterfly, too, and it was so big I thought it was a bird."

He remembered that, the image vivid against his closed eyelids: Lily as before, her hands and face sticky with melted ice cream; her eyes closed against the lengthening shadows; her mouth a thin, crimped line as she tried in vain not to cry.

"But," Lily went on, as bright and matter-of-fact as if those aspects of the day were far from her mind, "I wasn't down there very long before you came to get me, and you told me I was very brave to be in the park by myself. And then you picked me up so we could go home." She wedged herself more securely against his chest, the bones of her shoulders sharp even through the fabric of his shirt. "So it was a nice dream."

Aeris folded her tightly into his coat and, as her clicking laughter filled the hollow of the Tree, pressed a kiss against the top of her head. "I am happy for that, little one," he replied, and straightened with his eyes properly open. As his vision adjusted to the sudden influx of light, an unexpected sheet of white caught the corner of his eye, and he blinked—and blinked again.

Sometime during the night, the rain had turned to snow. A layer of it, as thin and fine as sand, blanketed the clearing. Atop the snow lay a final scattering of autumn leaves, each one dead and brown and drab even in the light of the risen sun.

Lily, oblivious to his stalled heart, picked at his sleeve with one claw. "I'd like to play pass-the-stone with everyone else now," she announced. "If that's okay."

"Yes, love. Go on." Aeris loosened his hold on her, not quite attending as she slipped out of his lap. "Play as long as you like."

"Dani! Dani, you're awake! Play with us!"

"No stalling, Mira! You have to guess."

"I don't want to guess yet."

"You gotta, my hand's getting tired."

"Children," Aeris began, and the bickering wavered. He looked at them, then, all of them seated in a ragged circle, shoulder to shoulder to shoulder, with Mira crouched in the center. "How long have you been awake?"

They exchanged glances. Min's flowered shoulders went up in a shrug, and Aimee answered with a soft, "I dunno," at the same time as Finn guessed, "A few minutes? An hour?"

"Two-hundred years." This from Sen, who grinned at the reproving glare Hori shot in her direction. "We've been awake *forever.*"

"You just woke up."

"No, *you* just woke up. *I've* been awake forever."

"You rolled over in your sleep and hit me in the face and woke yourself up."

"See, I'm right: y*ou* just woke up."

"Oh!" Ash's ears swiveled. "Someone's here."

Aeris lurched upright, his heart lodged unbeating in his throat. He needed to grow the thorns taller—twist them tighter. He'd slept too long—anyone might have crossed the barrier—anyone might have found him unconscious and his children undefended.

No. *No.* The visitor was William. *William* waited on the far side of the barrier, waving at them with the whole of his arm. Not a threat. Not a stranger.

With a whoop, Sen and Amaya took off across the clearing, carving a path through the newly-fallen snow. Aeris eased the claws from his hands and the brambles into less of a tangled web. William stepped through the resultant gap and managed to hop safely away from the thorns as Sen cannoned into his arms.

Aeris braced himself against the change in temperature and took one step beyond the Tree. Despite the sun, the cold cut through his clothes and skin and left him brittle, as easily snapped as a frozen twig. He drew in a breath, and the air rushed knife-sharp into his lungs.

William strode toward him, a breath of color in the grey-and-white of winter, Sen and Amaya bouncing puppy-like at his heels. June hurtled around Aeris's legs with a shout of welcome. Aeris took one step more as William reached him, and Aeris caught a flash of a grin and a glitter of gold before William's arms were around him, so unapologetically tight that Aeris could not breathe.

"Thank you." The words, warm and resonant, brushed his ear; William's hair, snow-dusted, tickled his cheek. "However you did it, thank you."

And then, before Aeris could reply or even raise his arms to respond in kind, William stepped back, and Aeris saw him properly and still could not breathe.

William *glowed*. Delicate threads of gold crisscrossed his cheeks and trailed onto his neck, as softly bright as ore in a stream. Aeris had ministered along those lines, had swept away dirt and clinging sap; the hash of scratches left by the brambles had metamorphosed into a tracery of gold beneath William's skin. And where before the deeper cut on his cheek had been half-scar and half-scab, now it flashed bright and molten along the curve of his cheekbone.

But even without the veins of gold, even without the new, splendid luminosity, William wore radiance like a crown. He stood close, breathless and flushed, his hands twisted into the fabric of Aeris's sleeves, his breath a plume of white between them, his eyes so bright with life they nearly burned. Aeris had not seen him before with such a blazing, unselfconscious grin.

"Look at you. William." With one finger, butterfly-soft, he touched the corner of William's mouth and marveled that he was not singed. He cupped William's face in his hands, tipped his head to better see the slivers of gold edging his jaw. The lines glinted, even when in shadow, and Aeris found them smooth against the pad of his thumb. "*Look* at you."

"I know, I know!" William clutched Aeris's sleeves, his wrists. "I woke up like this—I can't believe it."

William's voice, even as it shook with excitement, sounded deeper than before, and Aeris noticed, then, all the rest: a stronger line to William's jaw, a new broadness in his shoulders, his cheeks less round if not less soft.

"And this—this." William let go of Aeris's arm to press his hand against his chest. "I don't have to worry about-- about binding or *anything*."

Sen and Amaya tugged, one each, at the legs of William's jeans. "You changed, then? Did you change?" they asked, voices overlapping.

"Let me see, let me see!" June had seized the hem of his sweatshirt and was bouncing on her toes, trying to reach the nearer of William's hands. "I want to see!"

"Can you change into things like Dani can?"

"Oh!" Amaya drew in a delighted gasp. "Be a bird!"

"Be a bear!"

"No, be a *bird*."

"I want to *see*."

William stepped back with a laugh, and Aeris let him trail out of reach as he knelt, showed his hands back-and-front to June, let her catch his fingers. The wounds across his knuckles, halfway to being scars, had likewise healed bright and smooth: beaded amber trailed up his wrists and disappeared beneath the knit cuff of his sleeves.

"I don't think I can turn into animals," William admitted. He glanced briefly up at Aeris, still grinning, still rose-pink from the cold. Sen and Amaya had asked the question, but Aeris suspected this answer was for him. "I don't even know why *this* happened."

"You did not eat the fruit." A statement, not a question: Aeris already knew the answer.

Sure enough, William shook his head. "I didn't. I put it under my pillow last night, and it's still there."

"Eat it!" Amaya insisted, patting William's cheek with a paw. "Grow fangs! And fur and scales and horns!"

"All that at once?" William gave in to another laugh, the sound as warmly-bright as the scintillating gold beneath his skin. "That seems like too much."

Amaya continued to paw at William's face, and June bent and unbent his fingers, and Sen tried to hook a thumb around the corner of his mouth to see his teeth, and William bore it all with a lopsided grin and saintly patience, so relaxed and comfortable that Aeris could not quite believe this visitor was the same half-wild stray of early autumn.

Even with William's arms no longer around him, Aeris felt as if he had drawn a breath and could not let it out. He exhaled, but still his chest ached, as tight and sore as if he had swallowed more air than his lungs had room for. He crouched beside William and this cluster of his children, trying in vain to loosen the knot in his chest.

And then William shifted to look at him, and his hair caught the light as it always did, all threaded gold, and as William's mouth tilted into a wildfire smile, Aeris's thoughts spun toward raspberry honey and rosehip wine and brown sugar dusted over summer fruit—

Oh. *Oh. This* was William in summer—and he was beautiful.

"Thank you," William said again, soft and certain, and Aeris turned away, toward the Tree, uncomfortably warm despite the winter air.

"For what do you thank me?" he asked, too discomposed to disguise his disbelief. "Yours is a misplaced gratitude, for I have done nothing."

"This place is magic. Your family is magic. Thank you for insisting I be part of it."

Thank you. Thank you, as if Aeris—not William—gave the greater gift. *Thank you,* as if by accepting Aeris's mantle, William owed him a debt born of great and selfless sacrifice. The gratitude slid like a knife into Aeris's ribs. He, not William, owed the debt. He ought to be trading fairy gold and favors in exchange for William's acceptance.

"You have nothing to thank me for," he said again, stiff and formal and ashamed of how little he could offer in recompense. "The gratitude is all mine."

William laughed, unconvinced, and the knife twisted deeper. Aeris set his jaw against a rash reply, swallowed a rebuttal and his pride and every instinct in him that screamed for a fair trade. He could offer nothing else, and William wanted nothing else, so what did it matter, then, if the scales tilted thus?

"If you didn't eat, then how'd you get these lines?" Sen asked, and Aeris turned in time to see her pinch William's cheek and tug. "It's like you've got lightning in your skin."

"Or roots," June whispered, openly hopeful. "Maybe you'll grow flowers, too."

Someone clambered up the back of Aeris's coat to peer over his shoulder: Bri, her six extra eyes wide open in twin lines along her temples. "William's part of the family now?" she asked. "Even though he didn't eat?"

"Well, my love," Aeris began, as William turned his gaze, green and brown, upon him, "I have likewise eaten nothing, and yet I am family. If William does not eat, that signifies only that he is not hungry."

Bri's eyes blinked, one after the other. "So he's gonna be like you? Not like one of us?"

Beside him, William, previously still, tensed. His silence turned expectant, and Aeris, stealing a reluctant glance in his direction, read his question and his alarm in the lift of his eyebrows and the hike of his shoulders: *Do they not know?*

Those of his children with fur or feathers had picked their way out of the Tree, more interested in the new snow than William's arrival. They wrestled or hopped between footprints or burrowed between the roots of the Tree, but they were too close— all too close—and Aeris dare not answer, not even with the barest tilt of his head.

"Moreso like me than you, my dear," he said instead, and shrugged his shoulder, swinging Bri low enough for him to nest a kiss against the dark, bristling fur of her cheek. "He is here to help keep you out of trouble."

"Yesterday, *he* was the one who got into trouble." Sen managed at last to stick her fingers into William's mouth. She hauled up one corner of his lip to expose his molars. "So I think that makes him like us."

"Can we play again today?" Amaya asked, as William gently extricated Sen's hand from his mouth. "Can we play toss again? If we don't make a mess?"

"You may, if you like, but William is not dressed for this weather."

William's answering smile hung crooked and did not reach his eyes. "He's right," he admitted, catching Sen's other hand as she attempted to grab his chin. "It's too cold for me to play outside. I'm sorry."

Bri slid down Aeris's arm to drop into the snow, all eight eyes still on William. "Can't you grow fur?"

"We'll see. I like the shape I have now."

Aeris rose and adjusted the fall of his coat to avoid William's searching gaze. "Inside, then," he insisted. "You as well, Sen and June; neither were you built for the cold."

At the summons, June wobbled to her feet and tugged on William's sleeve to draw him up as well. Sen wriggled her hands free from William's grasp and hopped one step sideways to catch Aeris instead. The skin on her arms had lost its sandpaper roughness, and her fingertips were soft where they latched onto his wrist.

William stood, too, but took no step toward the Tree. He waited, Aeris knew, to speak with him a moment without the impediment of other listeners. *Do they not know?* But Aeris did not

136

want that conversation—not here, not now. He touched William's hand as he passed, but he did not linger as he stepped back inside the Tree.

As he crossed the threshold, heat sank into his bones and roosted like a bird in his chest. He did not realize how much the cold had sapped him until heat crept back into his fingertips as pins and needles. Behind him, he heard a small, startled exclamation from William as the young man followed him inside and, presumably, encountered the same effect.

Those of his children who had not ventured out into the snow sat still in a ring, the circle smaller now in the absence of some of the players. Only Mika lay asleep, Eris's blue luminescence casting a protective glow across his face. Mira, still in the center, glanced up at their arrival, and her gills flared in surprise.

"Oh!" she exclaimed. "You're all gold now!"

"Yes, he's fancy," Sen replied, before William could answer. She let go of Aeris's wrist and shook a warning finger in Mira's direction. "But he doesn't want to turn into animals now, so we're not supposed to ask him."

"I don't think I *can* turn into animals," William insisted. The Tree's warmth had brought a high color to his cheeks, his skin rosy beneath the freckles and new gold. As Aeris watched, William grasped the shoulders of his sweatshirt and hitched it up and over his head, then off completely. He wore a short-sleeved shirt underneath, as scarlet as autumn. Gold threaded up his arms, too—a branching, winding river across the map of his bare skin.

"Are you here to play inside games with us?" Sorrel asked as William slung the sweatshirt around his waist. "This one is pass-the-stone."

"How do you play?"

Mira's webbed hand shot upward. "I have to close my eyes and count to twenty. And then I have to guess who has the stone, otherwise I have to go again."

"You'll be good at it," Sorrel added. "You have hands."

"I dunno. You were all *really* good at catch."

"You should play with us. Sit!"

The children shuffled, widening the circle to leave a gap for William, but William did not move. He turned to Aeris, his silence a question and a challenge, and Aeris could only look back at him, anxiety a lightning shiver up his arms, the encroaching confession prickling like an incoming storm. *Do they not know?* William could ask, in front of as many listeners as he chose, and Aeris could not lie—not to anyone, not to his family—and he could not deflect, not with William in possession of the most volatile piece of the truth.

"For what do you look at me?" he asked, all innocence. "Be it your will that I join as well?" He bowed, deep and theatrical, with a hand pressed to his heart. "I am, my dear one, at the mercy of your discretion."

William flinched, then, and flushed a deeper red. "None of that," he muttered, trying and failing to match Aeris's nonchalance. "It's nothing."

The lie tasted ashen, even in someone else's mouth, but Aeris had his reprieve: William let tiny hands and claws tug at his clothes until he joined the circle. A flurry of voices assailed him with variations on the same three rules, and William listened, earnest and attentive.

With his guest suitably distracted, Aeris withdrew, as silent as a shadow, to the opposite side of the Tree's cavity. There, he found Mika sleeping still, Eris curled beside him, one arm tucked around the bundled baby and his forehead pressed against Mika's temple.

"He hasn't woken up yet," Eris whispered as Aeris drew closer. "And he still hasn't grown any horns or claws or anything."

Aeris crouched beside them and touched two fingers to Mika's forehead. No fever, no chill. No hitch in his breath or rattle in his chest. No reek of disease or infection.

Perhaps Mika had been rescued before he could begin to desire armor or camouflage. Perhaps Mika wanted only an attentive family—and in gaining one, he had no need for spikes or scales or new skin. Perhaps Mika's still-human shape signified nothing.

Perhaps.

Aeris turned his gaze, then, from Mika to Eris. "How fare you, firefly?" he asked, also in a whisper. He tucked a curl of Eris's dark hair behind a pointed ear. "Are you likewise so tired?"

"Yeah," Eris admitted. His eyelashes nearly brushed Mika's cheek as he closed his eyes and burrowed closer. "I don't want to play today."

"Not even in the snow?"

"Yuck." Eris shook his head, his hair whisking Mika's cheek. "It's cold and it's wet."

"Aye, it is," Aeris agreed. "You need not--"

A prickle at the back of his neck--

A sudden hush from his children outside--

The stink of spearmint searing ice-cold through his nose--

Aeris shot upright at once, twisting into fur and fangs and four legs. Those of his children inside had frozen, either at the smell or at Aeris's sudden movement. William alone startled to his feet, only to stumble back with a yelp as Aeris whipped past him.

The Tall Ones glinted in the sun, as hard and grey as flint, their skin pebbled with the first of their winter feathers. They shrank back with a collective hiss as Aeris slid a stop at the boundary in a spray of snow. But within a breath, they crowded forward again, as ugly and relentless as carrion birds.

Aeris flashed a row of razored fangs. "Get back." With his mouth so sharp and overfull, the words were nearly an incoherent snarl. "Go away."

"No." The nearest—nay, all of them—shook with scarcely-suppressed rage. Their wings shivered on their backs; their breath steamed. The nearest spoke again: "Did you think we would not know? Did you think we would not smell the difference?"

Their mockery Aeris had expected; their anger, he had not. Was this some new trick? "Of what am I thus accused?" he asked, bristling still, defensive still.

"You *infected* him," one answered, her voice the rasp of steel on steel. "You sully the Woods with such an aberration."

Aeris growled again, more in unease than in anger. "I have done no such thing, and to say I have is to lie."

She recoiled as if struck. "How dare you!" she hissed. A sibilant reproach rose from rest, and they surged forward near enough to prick themselves on the wall of thorns.

Aeris dug his claws into the snow and the earth beneath, sent a desperate *Grow* spiraling into the dirt and the existing barrier. Magic leeched out of him, as pitiful as a stream in drought, and twisted his heart until it ached.

But the brambles grew: new shoots, new leaves, new growth curling green and soft from the winter-blackened tangle. His legs wavered and vision swam, but the brambles grew.

"How dare you!" the same Tall One insisted again. "How dare you accuse *us* when evidence is in every *diseased* plant between us!" And before Aeris could flinch or protest or intervene, she seized one of the new shoots and wrenched it from the branch.

Aeris saw the tear, heard the snap, felt the break as a needle-sharp sting of pain and surprise. Golden sap welled at the rupture and dripped like blood down the Tall One's wrist, and Aeris realized at last where along the border they stood.

The brambles between them lay half-crushed, some of them broken entirely. The midnight rain had washed them clean, but yesterday, their thorns had been dark with sap and dried blood both. William's blood.

The slender cuts across William's face—the sap in his injuries—his blood smeared across the brambles—the gold beneath his skin.

"Wild," Aeris gasped, dizzy with understanding, dizzy with the brambles still sprouting new and green with the dregs of his magic. "He is Wild."

Another hiss rose—a climbing howl of disapproval. The Tall Ones tore at the barrier, heedless of the thorns or snagging branches, and Aeris recoiled, horrified and repulsed by their blind rage.

A streak of gold--

A shriek of outrage--

An animal—an eagle—huge and golden fell upon the Tall Ones like a brutal slash of lightning. Talons tore at their papery skin; a wicked hook of a beak sliced indiscriminate at faces and eyes and uplifted hands. The Tall Ones, screeching, tried to strike the bird's wings, feathers, face, but—as fast as a blink—the eagle changed. It spun from eagle to cat, scratching and spitting—to wolverine—to ferret, a slip of sunlight small enough to slither through the Tall Ones' grasping fingers—to eagle again, sweeping backward to Aeris's side of the border—

To William, who straightened beside Aeris, blazing and wild, his arms bleeding gold and his whole body tense with unspent energy. He was panting, each exhale a great cloud of vapor in the still air, but his attention was fierce and unwavering and fixed unerring on the creatures he had left scratched and seething. His

143

fingernails sparkled silver with the beaded mercury of the Tall Ones' blood, and Aeris relaxed, too exhausted and disoriented to better express his gratitude.

As the Tall Ones tried to ruffle themselves into some semblance of order, one managed a sneer at Aeris and William both. "This is a coward's trick, Aeris," he whispered, his voice dangerously soft. "Hiding like a child behind your half-feral dog."

"You assholes heard him before." William set a hand on Aeris's shoulder, bruised fingers curling possessively into his dark fur. "Fuck off."

Another rustling hiss rose from the Tall Ones. "Speak not so to *us*, foundling," one replied, her voice stilted with disdain. "You are nothing more than a human with soiled blood."

"*Fuck. Off.*"

William spoke without magic, but the conviction in his voice, the naked outrage, produced the same effect: the Tall Ones wavered a moment, all of them bleeding and bruised, then vanished one by one as if into a mist between the trees.

Not even when the last one faded out of sight did William soften. "Are they gone," he asked, his fingers still twisted tight into Aeris's fur, "or are they hiding?"

"They are gone."

"Will they come back?"

But Aeris did not have the strength to answer. His thoughts drifted, unfastened, to the ache in his chest, to the still-hungry scraps of new greenery pushing between the brambles. Dizziness swept through him in a wave, too strong a tide this time to fight against, and his knees buckled beneath him. William's face swam closer, bright and concerned, but Aeris's vision fuzzed and greyed and went black.

XVI

HE WOKE IN THE SNOW, his hands still clawed, his talons still scabbed with dirt. The wet cold of melted snow seeped into the fur along his ribs and his hind legs, but his shoulder and his cheek were warm. William, kneeling, had looped his arms around the animal barrel of Aeris's chest in a clumsy attempt to keep him from the snow; the frantic tattoo of his heart like a drum against Aeris's shoulder.

Fatigue left him hollowed-out, a damp rag twisted dry, and for a moment, Aeris closed his eyes again. William's embrace, though too tight, brought with it an easing warmth and steadiness, and the thrum of his heart, though too fast, felt like an invitation— an enticement to relax, to settle drowsy and tranquil into the reassurance of a pulse so near his own. He need not fight. He need not stay awake. He could sleep—and he wanted so much to sleep.

But he heard the snow-softened scramble of small feet and paws, and so he drew in a jolting breath and shivered into human form. William's grasp, previously a vice, loosened enough for Aeris to free himself. He managed to stand halfway before dizziness swept through him. He swayed and caught himself with a hand on William's shoulder.

"Don't move." William held his arms, his fingers as tight in the fabric of Aeris's coat as they had been in his fur. "Don't move."

The sky had turned grey, a sunless expanse of slate-colored clouds. Scents overlapped: the warm, soapy smell of William; June's vanilla-sweet flowers; the familiar wet-dog smell of Amaya's fur. The cuff of his coat was smeared with silver—starlight—blood from William's hands.

"They will come back," he whispered, too softly for anyone but William to hear. "They always come back."

William did not answer, but neither did he have a chance to reply. June reached them at a run and threw her arms around William's neck; Hori arrived a moment later and crashed into Aeris's chest.

Reflexively, Aeris pulled his coat over the small body fastened to his shirt, murmured, "It's alright, it's alright," against the curve of his little one's head. "They did not come in. They are gone. It's alright."

147

The rest of his children did not crowd so close. With Aeris on his feet and the Tall Ones out of sight, their alarm receded, as easily melted as snow in summer. Aeris felt them calm, felt the wash of trust and innocent confidence that swept away the last of their panic. Only Hori, burrowed against Aeris's neck, was not so swiftly mollified.

Only Hori—and William, who scanned the surrounding forest with a hunter's vigilance. Aeris could feel his agitation in the tightening twist of his hold, and with the one hand he had free, he eased one of William's from his sleeve, pressed the young man's fingers with the same reassurance he had given his children.

"Let us inside." As words and touch drew William's gaze, he added, still gentle, "They will not hasten back after such an assault."

William did not blink, and his grip did not lessen. His eyes were an eagle's: amber and flecked with gold.

"You *can* turn into animals!" Sen cannoned into William's ribs, startling a yelp out of June. "You said you couldn't!" she went on, too delighted to be truly hurt by the inveracity. "You were the *biggest* bird I've ever seen!"

William did not respond, nor did he seem to notice either of the children clinging to him. While his eyes remained upon Aeris, his attention seemed elsewhere—his gaze unfocused. His breathing, shallow and rapid from the fight, had not slowed, and his fingers were so tight upon Aeris's sleeve that Aeris could feel the fabric straining at the seams.

"Children," Aeris began, and though his voice remained gentle, his children stilled, at once attentive. "Return to the Tree, please. Wait inside."

Without a word in protest, they obeyed. June and Sen detached themselves from William and joined their siblings scampering back into the Tree. Hori gave Aeris's chin a parting nudge with his leathery nose, then retreated likewise.

Their audience gone, Aeris eased himself back down into the snow and knelt close enough to William that their knees touched. "You are going to breathe." He took William's hand, held it palm-flat against his own chest so William could feel the rise and fall of it. "Deep. And slow."

William's breath hitched—and did not ease. His pulse, strong against Aeris's palm, pounded still too fast. "What-- Aeris, what--"

"Deep," Aeris insisted again, "and slow."

"What the *fuck* were those things?"

"A court of carrion flies. Scavengers and parasites. Breathe."

"They're going to come back." William's voice cracked and darkened. "They're going to come back, and I'm going to kill them."

149

Aeris did not argue, only ran his thumb back and forth, back and forth across the ridge of William's knuckles. "They will not come back today, love. Not after that impressive intercession." He tilted his head, pleased to see William partially track the movement. "You wore so many shapes and in so short a span."

"I didn't mean to. Or want to. I just-- I saw those-- those things—and I saw you flinch—and then--" William blinked, as if with great effort, and his gaze seemed to settle, to roost more fully on his company. "I had to keep them from-- from hurting you. The rest, just... just happened."

From hurting *him*? Aeris leaned backward, surprise a sickening twist in his stomach. "From hurting *me*?" he asked, aware of and embarrassed by the untempered bewilderment in his voice. "You intervened for *me*?"

"Well, yeah." With another blink, William's eyes slid from swirling, inhuman gold to a familiar brown and green—neither one less piercing for the change. "Why are you--? Is that a surprise?"

From hurting *him*. William's protective ferocity had been for *him*. And William—his arms bare and bloody, his hair a tangled mess of copper—blazed with that fierceness still. So he had been from the beginning—fierce and bright and beautiful—and so he was now, if not more so, his skin split and seamed with gold as if he had not room in his body for all the light inside.

Aeris drew William's hand from his chest, amazed again that contact did not leave him scorched. William was a burning sun, and he a waning moon, and such a fire ought not be for him.

"Lionheart." He shook his head, his hair spilling dark and oil-smooth over his shoulder, and favored his counterpart with a small, apologetic smile. "Fight for the little ones. Fight for your family. Waste not your valor on me."

He expected a scoff, an easy dismissal, but William's expression shuttered, a candle blown out, and he turned away. "You know, I--" He broke off, his voice soft and bruised. "I don't think it's a waste."

Regret pulled, thick as taffy, at Aeris's heart. This fire was not for him; this light was not for him. "It is, William," he insisted, gentle but implacable. "You know it."

"I don't-- Aeris, I don't--" William's voice splintered, then, and the tumult of his breath and pulse, so newly held at bay, began again. He ducked his head, shoved the heels of his hands against his eyes. "Don't," he hissed, but whether the command was for himself or for Aeris, Aeris did not know. "Just don't."

"'Don't' what, my dear?"

But William only shook his head. He did not unbend, and Aeris regarded, for a moment, the curve to his back, the way he tried to hold himself still, utterly still, in a way far too familiar. As if every thought and instinct turned inward, toward containment and control and quiet, quiet, quiet.

"William." Slowly, slowly, he touched William's elbow, his wrist, his cheek. William said nothing still, but the tension in his shoulders eased—a minute softening—and so Aeris slid his arms around William's neck and nested a kiss in the thicket of his hair. "William," he began again, unruly curls tickling his nose and his cheek, "tell me what ails thee."

"It's nothing," William muttered. Clumsy, halting, he knocked his forehead against Aeris's collarbone. "I'm fine."

He was not fully Wild, then, if he could lie thusly. Aeris rested his chin on top of William's head and did not dispute his claim. He could see, across the clearing, the empty mouth of the Home Tree. Warm, flickering light and a ripple of laughter floated out from within. He closed his eyes again and, this time, left them so and settled into silence, into the banked fire against his chest and within the circle of his arms.

Snow began to fall again, the thick white flakes of it settling in swaths upon William's hair and bare arms. Snowflakes lighted like chips of starlight on Aeris's midnight clothes, melting far more slowly than they did on William's freckled skin. The sky stretched above them, grey and woolen and darkening fast.

Gradually, William's shoulders rose and fell with steadier breath. With one final, shaky exhale, he pulled away and raked back his hair with both hands. "Can you stand?" he asked, and while he looked tired—the skin around his eyes pink and drawn—he managed a commendable attempt at composure.

Aeris nodded. In unison, they pushed themselves up out of the snow, unbalanced as they unfolded, each exhausted in his turn but stable enough to keep his footing.

As Aeris straightened, William caught his hand. Even in the snow, even in the cold, his touch was warm. Though he ought to, Aeris did not withdraw. Without a word, fingers laced, they picked their way carefully through the snow, toward the light and soft laughter ahead.

Upon the threshold, Aeris let go of William's hand and stepped inside. As he tapped the snow off his boots, and as William did the same behind him with his shoes, Hori broke from his upside-down perch and landed on Aeris's chest, wedging himself once more beneath Aeris's coat and within the shelter of Aeris's raised arm. The rest of his children did not pause in their games, and Aeris could see at a glance how they had amused themselves in his absence.

Most had returned to their game of pass-the-stone, but a few crouched in a cluster some distance away. Finn held an old, tiny piece of black chalk in one four-fingered hand and he scratched the chiseled end of it across the smooth wooden floor. The surface beneath had been smeared ash-grey, and Aeris could see residue on other claws and fingers from the erasure of previous sketches.

"You forgot the antlers," Bri insisted, pointing. "Finn, you forgot to give him the antlers."

"I didn't forget, I'm doing them last."

"Okay, but don't forget to put 'em in."

"I won't forget."

"Finn, draw him with feathers and wings—and big, big eyes."

"It's Bri's turn right now, Poe. I'll draw yours next."

Finn set down the sliver of chalk and sat back, his dappled fur fluffed with evident pride. As Aeris stepped closer, William just behind, Finn glanced up and gestured two-handed at his finished drawing. "We're drawing you," he explained.

Indeed they were. Finn had drawn a simplified figure with branching sticks protruding from its head and smudged thumbprints for eyes. The long shadow of its body receded into a dusty scribble, and both of its crooked arms ended in three long, equally-crooked fingers.

"A remarkable likeness, darling."

At his shoulder, William took a step closer, and Aeris glanced over to see him with his arms halfway crossed, one hand spinning, spinning, spinning the beads of his brown-leather bracelet. He seemed neither surprised nor appalled, only thoughtful, as he studied the chalk drawing.

"Bri can't draw, so I was drawing for her." Finn touched a finger to the top of the figure's head. "These are your antlers."

"I couldn't remember what your legs looked like," Bri admitted. "I don't think you had any."

"Is that what he looks like?" William asked. His gaze slid sideways to snag upon Aeris's face. "When he's not human-shaped, I mean."

Your eyes were all fucked up last time. What did he look like now, even with a glamour? What could William see? Aeris tilted his head, noncommittal, and let his hair, unbound, fall like a curtain between them.

"Not all the time," Bri explained. "Just when he came to get me."

Beside her, Poe nodded, his eyes closed in remembrance. "When I saw him, he had eyes like lanterns, and he was like a shadow, all stretched out."

"Was he scary?"

Poe blinked, head askew. "No. 'Course not."

"Yeah, why would he be scary?" Finn paused in the midst of erasing his drawing to fix William with the same puzzled look. "I was glad he was there."

"Do *you* think he's scary?" Bri asked.

"No." The truth—a bright, resounding bell. "No, not at all."

"That's good. Poe, I can do yours now. Tell me what to draw."

"We thought you were going to be sick." Bri gestured at the mouth of the Tree, at the snow falling outside. "Are you okay? Did you throw up?"

"I didn't throw up." William, bless him, answered with endearing sobriety. "But turning into so many animals at once didn't feel good."

"You could do the thing Dani does and mix them together. Then you're only one thing at a time, but it's a really cool thing."

"Maybe." Out of the corner of his eye, Aeris could see William crouch, his elbows propped on his knees. Dried, golden blood crusted along his bare arms, but even wounded, even ragged, he seemed calm, composed of glowing embers rather than a bonfire. "I think I might need a rest first."

"You can watch the drawing if you want."

"Thank you. That sounds nice."

Interest refocused on the chalk and its wielder. Hori eased out from beneath Aeris's coat and dropped down to watch, but Aeris remained standing, cold despite the layers of his clothes and the warmth of the Tree. His palms and soles and chest still ached, the pain dull but insistent, as if magic for the barrier had been dragged out of his skin and bones.

Not yet. Not yet.

Aeris stepped around the drawing circle to fold himself down upon William's other side. Beside him, William shifted, first sideways to allow him space, then to likewise settle, cross-legged rather than crouched.

"His wings were bigger—like twice that big."

"Were they the feathery kind? Or the bat kind?"

"The feathery kind."

"Okay. They might end up looking kinda the same either way."

"That's fine, I like how you're drawing."

Amaya slid away from those playing pass-the-stone and curled up in Aeris's lap with her cheek on his knee. The children's easy chatter from one group and their intermittent laughter from the other smoothed over Aeris's disquiet like a balm, and he relaxed, his back against a tier of empty alcoves. William's shoulder nudged his; Amaya chewed on the edge of his coat; and Aeris, closing his eyes, could feel the rest of his family in a swirl around him—stars in a scattered constellation, bright lights aglow in an empty, cavernous firmament.

Even with snow gathering on their doorstep and the cold creeping in, here and now, in this narrow sliver of time, between the warmth and the laughter and the love, this was home.

XVII

AERIS SAT IN THE DARK and sifted through the Tree's occupants for any sign of what had woken him. Nothing made a sound, either within the Tree or without, except for the soft, synchronous breathing of twenty-odd children asleep. Nothing prickled or itched beneath his skin to signify another assault at the barrier.

A half-lit figure in the mouth of the Tree took Aeris a stuttering heartbeat to recognize, but the shape was William, his back against the curved wood, his shoulders tense, his face turned toward the snow and the veiled forest. The wild-lights of the Tree drifted above his head, a slow, nebulous crown lighting him gold and amber.

Outside, the snow fell in a slow, moonlit swirl, the silver flakes all that Aeris could see in the darkness beyond.

Someone stirred, half-awake, at the edge of Aeris's thoughts, their intent amorphous, and Aeris knew, then, what had awoken him. He rose, soundless, on newly-bare feet.

Tucked into her high alcove, Sen lay on her side, her eyes open but nearly black in the shadows. She had removed her necklace and held it loose in her hands, passing each tooth like a rosary bead between her fingers.

"Still awake, my dear?"

"Yeah." Sen's hands stilled, but she did not look up. "I don't feel tired yet."

"You seem thoughtful."

"Yeah."

Though she did not elaborate, Aeris did not reply. Sen's silence felt hungry, restless, and Aeris knew to wait, to leave space, to provide the parchment but leave her the pen.

When she did speak, her voice was small but steady: "Can I sit with you?"

"Of course, seedling."

She set her necklace on her pillow, slid to the edge of her alcove, and dropped into Aeris's waiting arms. Her hands now free, she clasped them around Aeris's neck and propped her cheek on his shoulder. The weight of her in his arms had grown so familiar, so much a piece of home, that Aeris had to resist the urge to hold her fast, to trap her against his chest as if that alone could forestall the inevitable.

But tadpoles lengthened into frogs, and cocoons spun into moths, and Sen wanted to sit, so Aeris sat. Sen resettled in his lap and nestled against him, warm from her own bed; Aeris drew his coat around her to keep her so and, as she still did not speak, rested his chin on the top of her head. He closed his eyes, soaking up her silence, and determined to imprint this moment, too, for all its impending sorrow, upon his memory.

And then, "Dani?" spoken so softly that, had he not been listening, he would not have heard her. "Can I ask you a big thing?"

"Of course, love."

"Would you be mad if I wanted to live somewhere else?"

"No, sweetling, I would not be mad." He pulled his coat more tightly around her in brief, bracing reassurance. "Where do you want to go?"

Sen hesitated, but all the days before, all the lost teeth and the softening of her sandpaper skin, had been building to this. "I want to go out there." She pointed, unwavering, at the mouth of the Tree, at the falling snow and the forest, past William not-quite-listening in the doorway. "I want two moms and a dog."

"I think that sounds lovely."

Another pause, this one shorter than those before, and then Sen slid out from beneath his chin and tilted her head back to gauge his expression. "Is it bad?" she asked. "Is wanting that a bad thing?"

"Oh, my dear, no, of course not." His voice faltered in the answer, thick with sorrow that she would even ask, that she would know so well what she wanted and still hesitate. Out of the corner of his eye, he saw William tilt his head as if to listen. "For you to want another family is a good thing—the *best* thing."

Sen nodded. "Finn was doing all those drawings, so I was thinking about that a little," she admitted, still thoughtful. Without her toothy smile, in the flickering light, she looked almost like a stranger. "About how much I'd wanted someone to come get me."

She had tumbled into his arms as if he were a last resort, as if she'd been equally willing to fall out the window and find no one there to catch her. She had wanted *away*, so away they went, Aeris sinking into the shadows as Sen burrowed into his coat, her arms tight around his neck and her heartbeat a rabbit-pulse against his chest.

"What do you think now, love?"

"I think it hurt, and it was bad." She drew in a steadying breath and, when she continued, Aeris could almost hear the echo of his own voice in her answer: "And it wasn't my fault that it happened. It wasn't my fault. I didn't do anything wrong."

Aeris nodded, his spoken reassurance as instinctive as an exhale: "You did nothing wrong."

"And I want to try again with a new family."

Her certainty sounded smooth, crystalline, and so Aeris loosened his hold, tapped her lightly, briefly on the nose. "You will be a dandelion seed, my darling," he whispered, as playful in tone as in action. "Wherever you drift, there will be home."

"A dandelion?" Sen wrinkled her nose. "I liked being a goblin."

"You made an excellent goblin. Human or goblin or seedling, your new family will be blessed beyond words to have you."

Sen's reply was a yawn. She squirmed, pulling up her legs to push her feet against the inside of his elbow, and Aeris shifted to cradle her in his arms as if she were a newborn baby. With a sleepy sigh, she rested her cheek against his arm.

"I'll miss being a goblin," she muttered. "And I'll miss you. I won't forget."

She *would* forget. In a new life, in a new home, she would remember none of this, not the Tree, not him, not her siblings. Perhaps she would, once in a rare while, feel a flicker of nostalgia for something lost, but she would not be able to pin to it a name or a shape or a person.

Aeris stood. Already, Sen's eyes were drifting closed. Already, her skin was feathering, turning fuzzy and blurred. He brushed a kiss against her forehead, holding his breath as he did so to keep from disrupting her shape.

"I won't forget," Sen promised again. She muttered something, sleepy and indistinct, then added, "I'm not tired."

The snow eddied over the threshold and around his feet. The wind stirred the trailing ends of his coat, drew him to the mouth of the Tree, whisked his bare ankles with a breath neither hot nor cold. William, at his feet, held still and silent, his mismatched eyes bright and unblinking.

"Sen," Aeris whispered, and Sen murmured a reply too soft to hear, and Aeris's heart twisted in his chest. "I love you dearly, little one."

Sen inhaled, almost as if about to wake again, but her eyes remained closed, her head a gentle weight against his arm. "Love you, too, Dani," she mumbled, and added, with a lethargic sort of stubbornness, "Not gonna forget."

"Beloved child." One final nudge, her cheek paper-thin against his. "Go on."

As he straightened, a filigree sweep of white curved across Sen's face and hands: traced petals that began to curl and fray. She let out a breath, and in the exhale, the wind and snow tame at Aeris's heels swirled up around the pair of them. The breeze caught at the curling edges of her skin, whisked her cheek into a spray of silvery filaments. Her hand, her arm, her shoulder followed, and in a heartbeat, she was gone, a flurry of petals swept away on the wind.

Aeris let out a breath of his own and slowly, deliberately, lowered his empty arms. He could feel, for a moment, the phantom weight of Sen warm against his chest, but that, too, faded, erased by the cold of the settling snow.

"Aeris?"

Not yet. He could not answer yet. Without moving, without breathing, Aeris imagined sorrow a pond, deep and smooth, frozen in a solid block of ice. Freeze it through, bury it deep, not here, not here, not here.

"Aeris?"

A frozen pond, ruffled snow. How easy, to pass a hand across and smooth away the indentations. Smooth and smooth and smooth.

William did not renew his question, and Aeris kept silent, kept still. He held his chin high, his eyes on the falling snow, his back tense and straight. Ruffled snow—brushed smooth. A tiny

165

stone dropped into a blue-black ocean, sinking, sinking, sinking out of sight and out of mind.

But William's silence itched, as insistent as an open wound, and Aeris, at last, attended him. The young man knelt, halfway to standing, as intent upon Aeris as he had been on the forest. Wild-lights swirled around him and caught the splintered gold upon his cheek, left him as softly aglow as a drowsing hearth.

With Aeris's attention on him, William sat properly and pulled his sleeves down over his hands. "Are you okay?" he asked, as gently as if he already knew the answer.

"What would you do," Aeris began, carefully neutral, "if I was not?"

"Do you want to talk about it?"

Aeris lifted a shoulder, feigning unconcern, and turned back toward the snow. "You are staying the night," he replied, too tired to attempt a more elegant deflection. "Why so?"

"Well, you-- you passed out almost as soon as you sat down, and I didn't want to wake you or, uh, leave with all your kids running around. By the time everyone was asleep, it was dark out and still snowing." Just visible in the corner of Aeris's eye, William shrugged, his nonchalance equally contrived. "Besides," he added, "I wouldn't be welcome if I went back looking like this."

This referring to, most likely, more than the rivulets of gold embedded in his skin. Aeris considered that, considered William, considered the house in the city with its winter coats hanging empty and untouchable while William shivered on the front step. How even that had been an improvement upon whatever came before.

He folded his legs beneath him, still slow, still deliberate, and knelt, not quite facing William and not quite close enough to touch. "How much did you hear?"

"Of the-- Of what you said to Sen? Most of it, I think."

"If she had come to you with the same, with, 'I want to go home' and 'I want to try again,' what would you have said?"

William's posture didn't change, not enough for Aeris to notice, but his breathing slowed, the shift too sudden to be unmediated. "It'd be a new home?" he asked, his voice strained and simmering.

"Yes. She is born again, into something new."

"That's alright, then. They don't--" William broke off, swallowed, tried again in a voice hardly any steadier: "They don't go back to what they left, do they?"

"Never." He spoke more sharply than intended, the edges of his words as rigid as his posture. "I do not think I would not let them go, if that was where they went."

"Can you do that? Not let them go?"

"I have never tried. I do not hold them here. Their return is the best course." Though true, the words still scraped his throat raw as he spoke them. "That is what I hope for all of them."

"Aeris, how… how many times have you done this?"

"Hundreds." His voice wavered on the word, and he drew in a deep, deliberate breath. "Hundreds," he began again. "Beyond that, I shall not count."

William did not reply, not at once. Aeris suspected, but did not turn to ascertain, that the young man watched him, his double vision dangerously perceptive. Aeris tilted his head, if only to loosen his hair, to hide his face.

Eventually, hushed, soft with sympathy: "That sounds lonely."

Yes. Aeris bit his tongue, horrified by his impulse to answer as such. He curled his fingers, sank his nails into his skin. He loved them, hurt and mending and whole, and even if they took great, broken pieces of his heart with them when they went, he would never be so selfish as to hold them here forever.

"Their return is the best course," he insisted again. "That is what I hope for all of them."

"You really love them a lot."

Something in William's voice pulled Aeris's heart into his throat. He did not want this. He did not want William gentle and insightful and inviting, as if he spoke to coax a wounded animal into the open.

But, "Of course I do," he replied, tense—unbearably so—in word and in posture. He shot a sidelong glance in William's direction. "You know that already."

Beside him, William drew his legs up to his chest, rested his cheek against the dome of one knee. "Yeah," he admitted, unabashed, "but I like seeing it. They're really lucky to have you."

Aeris did not attempt a reply. He fixed his eyes again upon the world outside, upon the unmoving blanket of fallen snow, and scrambled, desperate, to layer on another coat of icy resolve. A frozen pond, deep and smooth. Nothing else, nothing else. He would not miss Sen—he would not miss any of them—he would not, he would not, he would not.

"Aeris," William began, still gentle, as calm now as Aeris was unsteady, "Why haven't you told them?"

"I can't." He had not meant to answer as such—had not meant to answer at all—but when he tried to add an evasion, an excuse, *anything*, he could only say again, threadbare, "I can't."

"You told *me*."

169

"I told a stranger, and him out of necessity. To tell them would be-- would be to--" He broke off, his voice too thin, too sharp. "They are children, and their happiness is hard-won. I would not burden them with this."

"Aeris, they would *want* to know." William shifted, the blurred shape of him angling closer, and Aeris closed his eyes, refused to look at him. "They *love* you. Give them a chance to-- Oh!" A hand, light, upon his sleeve. "What's wrong?"

He exhaled—or tried to. But he was fracturing, aware, in panicked fits and starts, of thinning, snapping ice; of his hands in fists, his fingers too long, too brittle; of his chest, stiff and tight and unmoving as he tried to breathe. William's voice was gentle, so gentle, and Aeris clung to the façade of his calm, to the crumbling pieces of his mostly-human body, but the spell drifted like smoke through his fingers, and he was too scattered to catch or shape it.

"Are you--?" The hand gone from his sleeve. Upon his wrist instead. "Are you okay?"

The impossible softness of William's concern would have been enough, but his thumb brushed the edge of Aeris's hand, as gentle as his voice, and Aeris froze. *Are you okay?* Quiet and honest and heartfelt—and how easy, how dangerously *easy*, to admit *no, no, no,* he was not, he was breaking, his heart cracking open in his

chest and his skin warm, too warm, with the risk of eyes on him—
on his face, on his hands.

He froze—for an instant. A heartbeat. And then he
recoiled—tore free his hand—spun out of human shape, out of the
body threatening to fall apart, out of the skin that betrayed the
wavering timeline of his life.

"Wait--" William began, but Aeris had changed already,
had turned small and sleek and stumbling on skinny legs. He
ducked, but William did not reach for him, instead wrapped his
arms around his waist and held still, very still. Aeris crouched,
watching him, ears flat and fur on end, and William stared right
back, startled, the pupils of his mismatched eyes huge in the dark.

"Aeris, I'm sorry." The words reached him from far, far
away, muffled and nearly-drowned by the rush of blood in his ears.
"I-- I didn't-- I'm sorry if-- if I pushed you. I'm sorry."

He wanted to run. He *could* run. He could bolt from the
Tree and from William and return with daybreak, with the shield
of his children awake. He did not want to be seen; he did not want
to be known.

And yet--

And yet--

And yet William sat tense and quiet, cast in amber and
shadow and copper as he waited for Aeris's lead. "I'm sorry,"

escaped him again, his voice small and frightened, his guilt and sorrow so palpable that Aeris could taste it: hyacinth and juniper. He twisted his fingers into the fabric of his sweatshirt to keep them still as if conscious of how easily he might burn what he touched.

This would not hurt. The realization sank into Aeris, swift and suffusive, rainwater into parched soil. Honesty was so often a weapon, a knife handed hilt-first, but William would not hurt him—not with this. This would not hurt.

Slowly, as if moving too quickly would startle him out of his own conviction, Aeris settled his fur and rose from his crouch. This would not hurt. He closed his eyes. This would not hurt.

The fox shape clung to him like a second skin. Aeris exhaled, loosened the fur by degrees, eased it gently away, lowered the shield he had nearly forgotten how to set down. *Home.* Not fox, not raven, not human. *No shape but mine.* No glamour, no mask, no magic to cloud or confuse William's sight. *No shape but mine.*

William did not gasp or exclaim, but Aeris heard the short, cut-off sound of his surprise. And then, softly, so softly, "Oh."

Aeris kept his eyes closed. He did not need a mirror to know his own reflection. He knew, well enough, the animal length of his skull, too angular to be human; the dark scales ridging his chin and throat; the cracked, charcoal remnants of horns curving at his temples. And he had seen, only once, the atrophy of his own face, the image seared afterward onto the inside of his eyelids: the skin of his cheek caving in to expose his teeth and the bone of his jaw; decay turning his skin the flaking grey of wild mushrooms; lichen creeping around and into the gaping black hole of a not-quite-empty eye socket.

"Aeris," William began—and halted. He sounded neither disgusted nor frightened, but Aeris fought back a shiver nonetheless, suppressed the urge to retreat into a body whole and beautiful and passably healthy.

"No." Aeris blinked, kept his gaze fixed on his folded hands rather than on William. "In answer to your question, dear William: no."

William's hands appeared briefly in Aeris's line of sight, hovering and uncertain, as if poised to touch—but surely not, surely not. Aeris did not turn his palms upward, did not invite what had not been offered, and William retreated a moment later.

"Are you... supposed to look like this?" he asked.

"No."

"Does it hurt?"

Aeris's throat closed against a proper answer, but he shook his head.

Again, William's hands wavered into view. "May I....?" he began, and Aeris, weak, unfolded his hands, unfurled his thin and

173

crooked fingers. At once, William took his hand in both of his own, his touch warm and smooth and sure. Aeris expected an inspection, a turning this way and that of what he held, but William only brushed a thumb back and forth, back and forth over the rough skin of Aeris's palm, the gold threading his fingers bright against the dark, jagged silhouette of Aeris's hand. This was not, Aeris realized with a pulse of disbelief, a study; this was comfort.

"William." He slid his hand free, set it, cold and empty, in his lap. "You should not."

"Should not what?"

Should not care. Should not be kind. Should not waste a spark on a spent match. But, "Your role," he said instead, "is to be gentle with my children. You need not be so with me."

"Why not?" William sounded puzzled, almost hurt, and Aeris closed his eyes. "Why shouldn't I care about you?"

"You should not," he insisted again, ice cracking beneath his feet. "Look at me. I am rot and decay and nearly dead, and what a waste of your kindness to--"

"No. Aeris, no." Warm hands cupped his face, lifted his chin. "It's not a waste. Aeris. It's not a waste."

Aeris slowly opened his eyes, let his gaze be caught and pulled—pulled toward William and the wild-lights like drops of sunlight in his hair, his cheek splintered gold, his mismatched eyes

174

bright and deep and focused. William looking at him—at *him*—as if he were something rare and precious and wonderful.

"It *is*," Aeris insisted, soft and shattered, but William shook his head and drew closer, and Aeris felt the feather of his breath as he nudged a kiss against the ruined crater of his left eye.

"Did you forget?" William asked, leaning back no real distance at all. "I heard *you*. I came here to help *you*. I want to look after your kids, but I also want-- I'm also here for *you*."

Aeris did not answer. Even with William partially withdrawn, he could still feel the kiss, over and again, the ghost of contact a lingering warmth upon his skin. Present still were William's hands flush against his cheek and the line of his jaw and the smell, fainter after a day away, of stale bread and human city.

This did not hurt.

This did not hurt—and Aeris felt the internal snap of warming ice, every careful layer of frozen resolve melting, melting, melting, as slow but inexorable a thaw as snow in spring. Tears rose, and William smoothed away those that fell, unbearably gentle, and Aeris gave in and bowed forward and pushed his forehead against William's shoulder. This fire was not for him, this light was not for him, but he wanted—so *dearly* wanted—to stay close, to stay warm, to dissolve into someone else's care and kindness.

William, bless him, did not retreat. He shifted, but only to raise his arms and rest them loose across Aeris's back, and Aeris closed his eyes, ill with exhaustion and the strain of feeling too much—far too much—at once. His hands, in his lap again, he tucked inside his open coat, as much to hide them as to keep them warm.

"I--" He shouldn't, he shouldn't, he shouldn't, but-- "I am so tired."

The arms around him tightened. "Then sleep. I'll keep watch for a while."

Then sleep. Aeris nearly laughed. If only the remedy were so simple. But he kept his eyes closed all the same and buried his face into the soft, worn fabric of William's sweatshirt. William tilted his cheek against Aeris's hair, his breath a warm, tactile flutter.

"Is this okay?" William's voice, so close to his ear, even in a whisper, sounded loud in the silence. "Do you want me to let go?"

In answer to the latter, Aeris shook his head. William lapsed back into silence, then, and all Aeris heard after that was the soft, slow in-and-out of his steady breath and the background shuffle of his children asleep and dreaming.

This did not hurt. A knife, some scarred and rusted blade long buried, slid free from his chest, and he could breathe again, the last dregs of his resistance dripping through the useless cage of his ribs.

This did not hurt.

« « « » » »

Perhaps he did sleep: the next thing he knew was William shifting again, his shoulder dipping low beneath Aeris's cheek.

"Sorry," he whispered as Aeris drew back. "My arm was falling asleep."

Outside, the falling snow had stopped; the clearing was a white, unbroken expanse bathed still in moonlight and not the rosy glow of dawn. Nothing stirred.

Aeris felt, as before, stiff and hollow—and cold as William withdrew. Wild-lights settled on the shoulder that had so recently housed his cheek, and Aeris regarded the damp and rumpled fabric with a new, ill-fitting embarrassment. At a loss for what to say, he said nothing, only waved away the roosting lights and straightened the edge of William's hood.

William, either unconscious of Aeris's unease or gallantly pretending not to notice it, likewise tugged on the collar of Aeris's coat. "Can I ask about your horns?"

Aeris did not look up. "What of them?"

177

"Have they always been snapped off like that?"

"I know not. Why do you ask?"

"I dunno." The shoulder under his hand rose in an affected shrug. "I thought maybe that might have tied into you being sick."

Aeris's heart sank—not from the sentiment, but for the answer he would have to give. "William." Eyes up, lost at once in green and brown. "My dear. Do not hunt for such as that."

"For such as what?"

"For solutions to a riddle that has no answer."

"Maybe there *is* an answer." William curled his fingers more tightly into Aeris's collar, but his expression—calm, composed—did not change. "You're magic; this place is magic. There must be some way to stop you from dying."

Aeris almost smiled at that—*almost*, at least, with the side of his mouth not locked into a sepulchral grin. "You would stop the seasons turning?" he asked. "Or the moon from waning?"

"There must be *something*." Then, as if part of the same thought, "What about those things that attacked you? Maybe *they're* killing you."

"William." Aeris set his palm over William's heart, and William went still. "Stop. There is only this world and this its only circumstance: I will die, and you will take my place."

"No." A hand upon his, as steady and certain as his voice. "Aeris, no."

"William--"

"*No.* You told me to fight for my family. And I want-- I want--" William broke off, but he did not blink, did not drop his gaze. A quick, there-then-gone cant to his mouth betrayed the facade of his calm, and so Aeris did not interrupt, did not with a misplaced word shatter the thinning glass of this admission. His hand, pressed between William's palm and beating heart, caught the staggering rise of his pulse.

"You're the first person who's used my name," William went on, this time unpolished, this time in a voice crumbling at the edges. His gaze skated away, hitched on the distant trees outside. "My parents didn't want me around my niece. Like I was dangerous to her. Or *contagious.* And yet they wanted me to love them no matter what, no matter how much of *me* they wanted to change, how much—or how-- how *little*—of me they thought worth keeping.

"But *you.*" Eyes on his again, green and brown and bright, so bright. "Aeris, there's *so much* love here, and it's from *you.* It starts with *you.* Your kids have mushrooms and wings and extra eyes and whatever, and you love them *so much.* You don't pick and choose. You just *love*. That's beautiful. This *whole place* is beautiful."

Aeris slid his hand free from William's chest, tucked a strand of William's unruly curls behind an ear. "We try again." Gently, so gently. "In a different garden, we try again."

William hesitated. Then, slowly, carefully, he threaded his fingers through the silken curtain of Aeris's dark hair. "Thank you," he whispered, soft and sincere. "For everything." He swept a night-black strand behind one tall and pointed ear. "For letting me see you like this."

This gentleness. This reverence. Aeris's chest ached, with gratitude or with wanting, he did not know. He had left his hand upon William's cheek, the pad of his thumb warm against smooth gold and scattered freckles. William's mouth tilted again, one corner twisting into a crooked smile, and Aeris might have touched it, might have returned the gentle imprint of William's kiss, might in some other circumstance have tried to coax such a half-smile into summer radiance.

But his hand upon William's cheek was grey and splintered, his fingers more bone and bark than skin. Aeris returned his hand to his knee.

Another pause, this one heavier than the one before, and then, "Aeris--" in a different tone entirely, and Aeris did not dare look up, not with William's hand ghosting warm against his chin. "You told me to fight for my family. I want that to include you."

"I will still be here, after a fashion." He reached up and drew William's hand down to his lap. "My heart is in the little ones."

"A good place to keep it." William's fingers curled through his, undaunted by the flaking ridges of his skin. "Or, I guess, twenty-- twenty-three good places to keep it."

"Yes." Aeris closed his eyes, his chest an empty, echoing hollow. "They have the whole of it."

"The whole of it, huh? You didn't keep any for--" William broke off. His grip tightened. "That fruit you give them," he began, as if he had not been partway through saying something else. "It grows on the Tree?"

"Yes."

"But the Tree, it's... it's also you. Isn't it?"

Aeris glanced up, puzzled, but he could ascertain nothing from the sudden abstraction of William's expression. "Yes, it is."

"And the fruit, it's getting smaller?"

"Yes. For what reason do you ask?"

But William did not seem to hear the question. "*That's* why it looked like that," he whispered, his gaze elsewhere—on something Aeris could not see. "Holy shit. Holy *shit.*"

He withdrew, shifted his weight as if to stand, and Aeris's heart leapt into his throat. He seized William's wrist, arrested him mid-rise. "Wait." Unease crackled electric through his voice. "Where are you going?"

"It's that fruit—that's how I can help you. I'll be right back."

He *was* leaving. His skin feathered, broke into gold plumage, and Aeris—for one heart-stopping moment—saw him dissolve into motes of light—as thoroughly gone as Sen and her siblings before her.

Aeris blinked—and William knelt there intact, head-and-shoulders above him, his eyes an eagle's again: amber and gold. "William," he insisted, "stay here."

"I'll be *right* back."

"I do not want you to chase a fantasy." But more than that, even more than the ensuing heartache of one final shattered hope, Aeris did not want to be left empty-handed and alone in the dark. "I want you here."

"Aeris, listen. It's not-- It's *you*. *You* need to eat it." William tried to twist his arm free, but Aeris held him fast. "I'll be fast—I'll fly—you won't even know I'm gone."

"William." Aeris's voice cracked, and William stilled. "I beseech thee: stay."

182

William met his gaze, the gold in his eyes not so inhuman that Aeris could not see the sympathy in them. But, "Aeris," he insisted, his conviction like iron, and Aeris's heart sank, "you said time passes faster in the city. I don't want to be too late.

"You saved my life." He rested his untethered hand on Aeris's shoulder, his touch light and summer-warm. "Now I'm going to save yours. Trust me."

And before Aeris could protest anew, William pulled free, his wrist and hand wrenched from Aeris's grip. Something caught on Aeris's clawed fingers—caught and snagged and snapped—and then William was gone, a feathered streak of gold growing smaller and smaller in the predawn sky, and Aeris sat alone in the mouth of the Tree, the string of William's bracelet split and frayed in his hand, its silver beads scattering like late snowflakes into the clearing beyond.

XVIII

THE SUN RETURNED.

William did not.

Aeris watched the horizon turn white with the dawn. Color seeped into the sky: pink and rosy orange, then a grey, washed-out blue. He plucked at the scrap of yellow fabric still secure around his wrist. With its counterpart severed, it served no purpose, but he could not yet bring himself to remove it.

The weak, watery light of the morning did little to unroost the settled cold from his body. He ached all through, from the weather as well as some other, heavier hollowness. And exhaustion, of course, plagued him still, as cumbersome and oppressive as a woolen overcoat in high summer.

The light of the risen sun, caught between the trees, glittered on translucent wings brittle and motionless in the cold. The Tall Ones never hunted before noon, yet they gathered now.

Perhaps there had been no possible end but this. Perhaps William had been an impossible hope from the beginning. He might return after one day, or he might return after two-thousand. Either way, Aeris would not see him again.

With a final glance at the trees and the converging Tall Ones, Aeris shed his coat and levered himself upright. His legs resisted after so long without moving, but Aeris pushed away the dissent, gathered up the scattered pieces of his resolve, and steeled himself for this last morning.

None of his children were yet awake, save two: Aimee and Finn drifted on the edge of wakefulness, tangled together in a kittenish pile of fur and too-long legs. Aimee stretched as Aeris approached and blinked, uncomprehending, up at him.

"Sleep a while longer, little rabbit."

Aimee rubbed a paw over her eyes. "But 'm not tired," she protested. Beside her, Finn shifted and wedged a hoof underneath her chin.

"It is not yet time to wake, love. *Sleep*."

Sleep.

Aimee's eyes fluttered closed. *Sleep* again, and Aeris cast the net wider, drew in even those still slumbering fast. *Sleep*, and he thickened the air, stirred it slow and stifling. From every alcove and pile of blankets, heartbeats staggered, nearly stopped. He heard their breathing snag on the spell, then soften to a whisper.

Sleep, deeper than hibernation—a hair's-breadth from an unwakeable rest.

Sleep. Until they could safely rise without him, without any guardian at all.

His skin prickled. He felt, but did not look to see, the Tall Ones outside, their fingers testing the dirt, seeking out infirm root and stalk. Theirs was a hesitant invasion so far—each of the foremost expecting reprisal. But William was not here to chase them away, and Aeris would not spend the last of his magic there.

Sleep dragged at him, too, an abyssal pull, but not yet, not yet. He rolled back his sleeves and set his hands flat against the inner curve of the Home Tree. "Whatever you need. Please." He rested his forehead, too, against the smooth wood. "Magic or strength or life itself. Take it."

Take it.

The wood split and cracked beneath his hands, and his fingernails sank into the softer skin beneath. Something dark and wet—blood or sap—welled beneath his fingertips and trickled down his wrists. Revulsion stuck in his throat and his stomach lurched, but he did not recoil. He could feel a heartbeat against his palm, a weak and distant flutter.

The mouth of the Tree began to close—the wood creeping layer by thin, crackling layer around the edge of the opening. Too slow, too slow: the Tall Ones' attention snapped toward the change. Their rustling voices rose like a gathering of storm winds.

Take it, Aeris insisted again. *Take me. Save them.*

Mushrooms raced up his arms, grey and swollen, their roots threading over and into his skin. Aeris bent one elbow and, as easily as if into water, sank his right arm into the body of the Tree. For a moment, he felt the cloying, soaking chill of mud on his sleeve, on his bare wrist—and then, abruptly, he lost all sense of his arm at all. Dizziness slammed into him and knocked the wind out of his lungs. He dropped, gasping, to his knees, prone but for the Tree at his shoulder.

Pain prickled in his left hand and along his remaining arm. Distant, stinging—the Tall Ones tearing at the barrier in a sudden, frantic advance. Thin, worming fingers ripped leaves, snapped branches, tore at buried roots. The sting of their assault turned sharp—biting—burning—searing up his arm and into his chest— flooded, scorching, through the rest of him.

His hand—his shoulder—pressed against a deep, grasping hunger, and it pulled at him, at his body and what shreds remained of his magic, and—thoughtless, desperate—Aeris let it pull, let it take and take and take. His vision swam, but he could see the mouth of the Tree closing, closing, the breadth of it too small a passage now for anything but a mouse.

His heart beat too fast, too shallow, and he was choking, drowning in the reek of rotting wood. But he needed a fortress—a stronghold safe from every outside danger. Blood or black sap soaked his collar and his sleeve and cooled the rampant fire that so swallowed the rest of him. He could do this. He could do this.

Save them one final time. A plea, a prayer, a threadbare spell as the last of his magic bled unchecked from his hand and his shoulder and his stumbling heart. His vision cut—and he heard for one moment the rattle of his own breath—felt the cold of the Tree seeping into his chest—tasted ice on his tongue. Then the cold sharpened to a scream—and darkness drowned the rest.

Aeris

Aeris

What...

What...

What did you do?

iron, sharp and wet—

      his teeth, his cheek

      upon his tongue

blood?

      no

      bitten fruit

          "Please, please, *please*."

                    "Please let this work."

white

wrinkled

      —worms.

Eating?   Eating him.

cracks in his skin

Gold—

    a flash

          then gone

    a shriek of rage

dirt in his mouth

    in his lungs

earth above him

earth below

    a choking blanket

Dying, dying, dying—

help me help me helpmehelpme

                            Sleep.

"He's not dead yet, so y'all can *fuck off*."

"Keep him, half-blood. Give us his flock, and we will go."

"*Fuck. Off.*"

bones jumbled in roots

a heartbeat   slow   slow   slow

wind in the leaves

A fluttering:

        early morning

        someone awake and wondering

"...has happened before?"

"kind of"　　　"not this long"

"he's so small"

"He'll be okay."

He crouched, trembling, his throat burning with the labor of breathing. Rain plastered his hair to his skin and drowned out any sounds of pursuit. His heart hammered in his chest, so hard and fast it hurt. He had to stop. He had to keep going.

He took one step and collapsed, mud soaking what was not already saturated by the storm. Too tired to run, too tired to stand. He had to keep going.

Footsteps—or the echo of them—pounded in his ears. He closed his eyes. *Please. I can't-- Please.* His heart lodged in his throat. They would find him here in the dark: small and skinny and well-past shivering. *Please.*

Please.

Please.

"Go on, you creepy bastards, give it a try. One step closer, and I'll snap your wiry little fingers."

"Tell 'em, Will!"

"Tell 'em to fuck off!"

"Oh! That's-- Don't use that word, okay? Let's not use that one."

His stammering heartbeat.

The rasp of his breath.

Nothing to see—nothing to feel—no world but this:

       a universe of *him*

              his heart, his body.

A tendril of   curiosity   concern?   against the bubble of his thoughts.

      He went still.

Had gone still.

    This: a universe of *him*—

               no—

                  a universe of *this*.

                     This great curiosity

                     sentinel

                        sovereign

    The world tilted

he fell

small, so small, a darting silver fish in the shadow of a passing whale

a seed dropped at the roots of an ancient tree

wind in the leaves

silva

silva

silva

WAKE

We all measure your time, and it shortens.

What are you?

The forest spat you out, and it will swallow you up.

Your magic is small, princeling.

Are you okay?

I heard you.

W A K E

Roots in his ribcage, closing around his heart

outside himself—inside himself

W A K E

He felt them as they skirted the edge of the clearing. An itch beneath his skin.

The Tree. The clearing. The ragged gorse ringing its perimeter.

Within, William and the children slept.

The Tall Ones sensed him and froze. *Princeling*, one began, hesitant, wary. *Standing at the feet of Death herself. Have you teeth to bite, or only dead and dusty words?*

Go. He stretched, felt them retreat from the touch of his mind. *Get thee gone.*

We will not go. These Woods are ours, and we will see the end of you.

No. The thought sparked unbidden, certain. They were wrong, though they believed the truth of it. No.

No—but why not?

why not?

why not?

why not?

his heart—beating

roots tangled through his ribs

an old body—

a darting silver fish

his heart

a seed

a whale

the world

the Tree

The Tree. The clearing. The ragged gorse.

I am the guardian of this place.

A rustling, rasping laugh. *Of the dead tree and the weeds?*

No. Of the Tree and the clearing and the gorse and—

wind in the leaves

silva silva silva

—beyond.

W   A   K   E

The trees, ancient and scattered—spring coiled sleeping in seeds beneath the surface of the earth—a sprawling tangle of roots above and below—the forest a branching, breathing web—and Aeris unfurled into this new shape, not into a body but into fullness, into a calling familiar but newly-remembered.

No.

No? The Tall Ones shifted, uneasy but defiant still. *Do you abdicate, then, princeling?*

You call me princeling, but you are not of my court. Pale and hungry—termites poisoning healthy wood, eating their way through to the heart. *You are not of my court, and you will go.*

Aeris, one insisted, commanding, but that was not his truest name, not with the whole of the Woods in his blood, and he would not be thusly bound.

No longer will you torment me and mine. He unfolded, as broad and deep as the forest and unshakably certain of his own mantle. *I am of the Woods, and I am of the Wild, and you have no power here. Begone.*

They resisted, stubborn and clinging—leeches and fleas to the last—but power and energy surged through him, more magic than his mostly-mortal body would ever have been able to hold. Fresh brambles exploded up through the earth, tearing at wings and legs as the Tall Ones scrambled backward. He was Wild, and he was of the Woods, and he would not forget again.

Begone.

Golden fur brushed his cheek. A feather-duster tail had swept around the slight, shadowy globe of his body, and he lay nestled against a cloud of sunset-orange.

All around him, in pairs, in piles, on heaped pillows and blankets, lay his children asleep. Someone pushed a warm, dry nose against his shoulder.

Everything tranquil; everything still. Aeris closed his eyes, awash in peace. A purr, not his, rumbled in his chest like distant thunder.

Sun on his leaves, on his face.
A northbound breeze against the bulwark of his body.
His family cradled in his hands, in his chest.

XX

WARMTH AND STILLNESS. The surface of an unruffled pond, its water smooth and undisturbed. He could, if he wanted, dissolve back into sleep, into the faraway, floating peace of perfect rest.

Laughter—a quick, distant burst of it—followed by the murmur of a calm, quiet voice. He opened his eyes. Sunlight poured into the Home Tree and lit the wood a gleaming honey-gold. The dome of the ceiling slid into focus, as polished as the inner curve of a bell. The air smelled warm and sweet.

He brought his hand to his chest. Past the open collar of his shirt, he could feel the smooth, near-human softness of the skin beneath. His heart beat steady against his palm—a strong and solid pulse, so far distant from the ghostly flutter of before that such frailty seemed like a terrible, receding dream.

"So it goes, 'A hat, a shoe, a glove'?"

"No, no, no! It's hat, shoe, belt, glove, shirt."

"Oh, I see. Hat, shirt, belt--"

This met with a flurry of indignant disapproval and another peal of laughter. But he knew that voice, knew that teasingly-serious tone.

He sat up. A gentle gust of wind scattered a handful of petals across the floor, stirred them like sparks around his bare feet and across his breeches. He had never seen petals like these: small and silken and so rich a saffron they might have been scraps of sunset. Someone had placed his coat like a blanket across his legs. Flowers and twigs stuck out of its pockets, most of former gold, the latter black.

The Tree was empty.

How long had he slept? What, finally, had woken him?

He rose, unsteady—and held his balance with the empty alcoves at his shoulder. At the movement, new petals cascaded onto his shoulders. He reached up, and even before his fingers grazed his temples, he knew what he would find: unbroken, branching antlers rising rough and wood-grained through his hair. They shed golden petals into his palm, and he could feel the smaller tines sprouting leaves and soft new growth.

A mantle. A forgotten crown.

And his arm—his *arm*. The fingers of his right hand bore the same whorls and shallow ridges as the surface of a young tree. He pushed back the sleeve of his shirt, and the bark continued past his wrist and along his arm and, presumably, all the way to his shoulder.

He could recall, vaguely, the seeping cold as he plunged it into the Tree, the visceral shock of its disappearance. He closed his hand into a fist, watched the shift of light upon his knuckles as his fingers bent with an ease and smoothness belied by their texture.

"Why are shoes the second verse? Why don't they go last?"

"Because that's how you get dressed. You put them on *after* you put on your hat."

Slowly, on legs unaccustomed to his weight but ready to bear it, he crossed to the threshold and stepped outside.

The clearing glowed, sunlit and emerald. Sunlight dappled the grass and spun falling petals into gleaming drops of light. The Home Tree's branches spread over the clearing like a great awning, its canopy a profusion of flowers and copper leaves and slivers of blue sky. Ringing the boundary, the brambles rose in a great tangle, rising toward and almost touching the Tree's outermost boughs. Flowers and leaves raced along the branches, and even from the ground, he could see the shape of their petals, their color the same as those still dusting his shoulders and clinging to his shirt.

The Tree. The gorse. Flowering—alive.

And the forest--

Overhead, the downy globes of pollen-coated bees zipped audibly from one blossom to the next. But he heard, too, on the distant edge of sound, a rabbit scraping in her burrow, a fox nosing through the underbrush, seeds unfurling in the dark beneath the soil. Life hummed in the backdrop of his thoughts, in his fingertips, as constant but quiet as the beat of his own heart.

Another laugh drew him back, and Aeris turned.

His family had not yet noticed him. They clustered around William, some of them wrestling, some of them drowsing in the grass, some of them pulling on William's hands and clothes in an escalating bid for his attention. All of them safe, all of them beautiful. Amaya chewing on the hem of the sweatshirt tied around William's waist; Bri dangling precariously from one of William's outstretched arms; Mika and Finn folded in William's lap and, somehow, fast asleep. And William himself, all sun and summer brightness, golden petals caught in his copper hair.

"Just one shoe?" he asked, his grin a teasing one. "Or do we sing that verse twice?"

"No, just once, otherwise the song takes too long."

William nodded. He began to reply, but his gaze caught on Aeris quiet in the threshold, and he went still. And Aeris felt again—briefly, vividly—the hand upon his shoulder before William left, the rending snap of the leather bracelet upon his claws.

William's audience turned to see what had thus snagged his attention, and the ensuing stillness and surprise lasted for one beat of Aeris's heart before it shattered into a sweeping joy so strong and sudden that he lost his breath.

"Dani!"

"Dani! You're awake!"

He did not reply, only opened his arms, and as the first of them—Hori—cannoned into him and burrowed a dry, wrinkled nose into his neck, he squeezed him so tightly against his chest that Hori laughed at the pressure of it.

"Dani! You slept so long!"

"We missed you!"

"We missed you *so much*!"

"It's been *ages*!"

Aeris dropped to his knees in the grass. Lily and Sorrel and Pel and Min squirmed into his arms, and he felt Bess land feathered on his back and Poe butt his forehead against his hip, and he laughed, lost in a delightful barrage of feathers and fur and grasping hands.

"I love you," he whispered. Then, more loudly, loud enough for all of them to hear, "I love you, and I missed you, and I am so, so sorry to have left you."

"Will said you were sick." Hori clawed his way onto the quieter perch of Aeris's shoulder. "He said you gave so much of yourself away that you didn't have any left for *you*."

"Yeah," Aimee put in, her paws on Aeris's knee. "You should have told us that you felt bad."

"I *am* sorry, dear ones." Even now, even safely awake, sorrow hitched in his throat. "I did not want to worry you."

"You always want us to tell you when *we* feel bad," Hori protested. "So you have to tell *us*, too."

"Are you okay now?" This from Finn, crouched within the shelter of Aeris's coat. "Do you feel better?"

"Yes." He answered without thinking and realized in the speaking that the sentiment was true. He felt loose and warm and settled—as if he had eaten a full meal but the sustenance had gone not to his stomach but to his heart. His chest did not ache, either with cold or with its old, gnawing emptiness.

He felt *awake.*

"Yes," he said again, resonant with the truth of it. "Yes, love. I feel much better."

"Good."

"If you need to, though," Sorrel began, "you can turn into a kitten again. We'll keep you safe, us and Will."

"Thank you, my dear." Aeris did not look at William, did not know what expression the young man might have nor what he hoped to see. "William looked after you, did he?"

"Yeah! He scared off the Tall Ones and told them to fuck off!"

"Oh?" Aeris tried not to smile, and he very deliberately kept his eyes on Pel, who had sworn so enthusiastically, as he asked, "And *did* that scare them away?"

"Yeah! They haven't come back in *so long*."

"And he'll turn into animals if we ask him nice!"

"And he knew you'd wake up, we just had to let you sleep."

"I told him we eat dirt, and he believed me!"

"And look! Look!" June wriggled her way to the front of the group and raised her hands, fingers splayed. "Look!"

Aeris's breath caught, even before June curled her fingers around his, the bare skin of her knuckles smooth and unmarked. Gone were the moss and white flowers; gone was the fractured and fragile patchwork of scars across her skin. As June squeezed his fingers, he could feel the new strength of hers, the proper healing of bones that had been, once upon a time, too broken to realign.

"Will said his scars, when he had 'em, didn't hurt him to see," June explained. "They'd remind him how he'd been hurt, but also how he'd gotten through being hurt. He said they showed him

211

what he could heal from. I thought mine could be like that, too, but they've been going all the way away instead."

Aeris brushed his thumb across the back of her hand. She had grown the moss and flowers so quickly, a riot of beauty to shield wounds too painful to see. "My darling, look at you." Love and pride lodged in his throat. "*Look* at you."

June squeezed his fingers again, her delight a frisson of joy in Aeris's chest. "Will is really nice," she whispered. "And it's okay that he's bad at singing the shoe song."

"He's bad at singing at *all*," Pel added, his voice conspiratorially low, "but we decided we're not gonna tell him that 'cause we like him singing with us. And we missed your lullabies."

June released his hands, so Aeris placed one solemnly over his heart. "I shall say nothing to him of his singing, whatever the quality," he promised, "but I would like to speak with him for a moment. Alone, if I may."

His children scrambled backwards to allow him space to stand, and those clinging to his back and arms dropped off as he rose. Pel, landing on his shoulder, hissed another, "Don't tell him about the singing," before he took off in a whir of iridescent wings.

William had not moved from where Aeris had first seen him. He stood now, barefoot in the grass, Mika cradled in his arms with the easy surety of much practice. As Aeris approached, he drew in a breath and opened his mouth as if to speak, only to close it without a word.

Aeris drew to a halt just beyond his reach, and they regarded each other in a moment's silence, Aeris with his head listed to one side, a smile tucked in the corner of his mouth; William with petals in his hair and freckles dusted across his bare shoulders and his mismatched eyes fixed upon Aeris as if upon a long-awaited sunrise—as if he was, still, something rare and precious and wonderful.

"Here," William began, and closed the distance between them. Aeris held out his hands without thinking, and William eased Mika into his waiting arms. "I think he missed you."

Aeris had missed *him*: the infant's solid weight against his chest; the huge brown eyes half-lidded, sleepy and unbothered. Tiny feathers sprouted along his hairline, and his curled fingers ended in pinprick claws, the miniature beginnings of an owl's plumage and talons.

And William—Aeris turned his gaze upon him. William had withdrawn no distance; he stood so close that Aeris could have swept the errant petals from his hair. He looked different, somehow: no taller, no broader, but holding himself so, as if his body fit him better, as if his newfound sense of physical comfort had matured into a deeper peace. *This* William was older, someone familiar and yet a stranger.

William pretended not to notice this inspection. He tugged on a misplaced curl of Mika's hair as if the baby still occupied the whole of his attention. "I missed you, too," he admitted, his voice soft and almost shy.

"The children seem quite taken with you."

"They were good," William answered, still without looking up. "I mean, they did tell me you let them stay up for all hours— *and* eat dirt—and I still can't convince them to stop saying-- to stop using curse words, but... but they were good."

"June is molting."

"Yeah. I was worried she would leave before you woke up."

Aeris tilted his head. Fragments of memory glowed like embers in the back of his mind: a sense of warmth and care, not from him but from his children; a purr, likewise not his, rumbling in his chest; the sharp, metallic taste of fruit on his tongue.

Somewhere else in the Woods, a flock of waterfowl skated onto the surface of a lake, feathers ruffling. A pair of fawns slept, nestled together, beneath the shelter of a fern's arching fronds. Wind whispered through branches and leaves and grass and blooming wildflowers.

Sleep, William had said. *I'll keep watch for a while.*

Sleep, William had said. And Aeris had slept.

"You were right." He cradled Mika with his left arm and reached up to pluck a stray petal from William's hair. "About the fruit. You saved my life."

William straightened, then, but still did not step away. As Aeris began to lower his hand, William caught it in one of his, his touch as light and careful as if catching a butterfly. He drew Aeris's hand closer and brushed his thumb along the striated curve of his wrist. "Is this okay?" he asked, examining the living wood of his skin.

Which did he ask after, the contact or the condition of his arm? "Yes," Aeris replied, answering both. He turned his wrist and wove his fingers through William's. "Quite so."

He had hoped for a smile, new sparks of a wildfire grin, but, "I'm sorry," William admitted, solemn and sincere. "You asked me to stay with you, and I didn't. If I hadn't been in such a hurry, you wouldn't have had to-- and I wouldn't-- I wouldn't have ruined everything."

Despite William's sobriety, Aeris laughed. "*Everything*, my dear William?" he asked. "What have you ruined? Show me."

William shot him a glance, doubt in the downturned line of his mouth. "I hurt you."

"You did." Aeris tightened his hold on William's hand. "I did not, then, want a cure. I wanted company. Had you not returned, we might speak of ruin, but my children are safe and well, as is their home. As am *I*—and all of that is thanks to you."

"You don't have to thank me for that."

"I do." Aeris extricated his hand, then, and placed it flat upon his chest. "You gave me back what I gave you freely and what little there was left of my spirit. For that, and for your service to me and mine, I thank you most deeply."

"You don't *have* to," William muttered, pink beneath his freckles. "Just keep a piece of your heart for yourself next time."

"Certainly." Aeris tilted his head again, ducked to catch William's newly-averted gaze. "But giving it to you was no mistake."

William made a cut-off, embarrassed noise. Upon the edges of his mouth flickered the start of the hoped-for smile. "Nice try, but you gave it to me so I could *eat* it. That's a bit less charming than you make it sound."

But Aeris had not intended to be charming. He brushed a hand into William's hair, let the strands curl loose and golden around his fingers. "It would seem," he began slowly, softly-spoken, "that I no longer need a replacement. But I want you to stay. The children, I am certain, want you to stay." He tucked an errant curl behind William's ear. "What, dear heart, do *you* want?"

216

"To stay." Eyes on his, green and brown and gleaming. "Of course I want to stay."

"Then 'tis settled." He rested his fingertips against William's cheek, and William exhaled a steadying breath. "Welcome home."

That earned a gentle, sunlit smile, and Aeris's heart twisted. He wanted to cup William's face in his hands and breathe his smile to brighter life, to commit to tactile memory the shape of it, the feel of it. He brushed his thumb against the corner of William's mouth, a silent question, and William's smile flickered.

"This is okay?" William asked, blinking up at him, his voice impossibly soft and hopeful. "Kissing is okay?"

"Quite so."

"Only I know you don't--" William broke off, turning red. "I know you don't like sex, and if kissing was off-limits, too, that'd be okay. I don't want to push you or make--"

But Aeris had already tipped into the kiss, into William's surprise and delight and, then, wonderfully, his gentle reciprocation, the soft returning press of a smile against his own. A hand settled light upon his cheek, and Aeris closed his eyes and sank for one moment, one slow, serene moment, into sunlight and stillness and the honeyed peace of William warm and close and sweet.

And then, "I have a shoe, a shoe, a shoe," reached him from the other side of the Tree, a disorganized chorus of voices more enthusiastic than skillful, and Aeris broke away.

"Quite so," he insisted again. And there—the smile he so wanted: the wildfire race of a grin across William's mouth. "Especially if you smile so after each one."

"Charmer," William muttered, falsely chiding, and his smile did not abate as he turned toward the sound of children in ragged harmony. "I mean it, though. Keep a piece of your heart for yourself next time."

With William's attention elsewhere, Aeris studied him for a clandestine moment. He glowed in the sun, the gold of his threaded skin so like the gold of the falling petals, the fissured light of him half human, half Wild, entirely radiant.

Aeris did not fear another winter as dark as the one behind him, not with the Woods in his blood and the clearing wreathed in spring and this heart alongside his, fierce and bright and achingly beautiful.

"I shall keep a piece of it," he promised. With a crooked smile, he turned toward the Tree and their children, Mika asleep in the cradle of his arms, and propped his shoulder against William's. "The rest is where 'tis beloved."

Acknowledgements

Thank you, Hannah, for being such a supportive friend and supportive reader. This one wouldn't be the same without you.

Thank you to the 2014-2015 student body of Northrop Elementary, especially the kindergarteners. You were a weird and wonderful pack of children; may you grow into weird and wonderful adults.

And thank you to the cast and crew of the 1986 Jim Henson film, *Labyrinth*. Aeris's character is a patchwork of many sources, but the first of them is a scrap of lace from Jareth's sleeve.

About the Author

E. Wambheim live and works in Minneapolis, MN, and is the author of multiple works centering asexual characters and gentle, loving relationships. When not writing, E works fulltime at a library, watches delightfully awful movies with a most excellent roommate, plays video games (somewhat poorly), and cannot stop buying plants.

If you have any questions or comments, please get in touch!

Twitter: @EWambheim
Email: ewambh@gmail.com
Website: https://ewambheim.wordpress.com

About the Author